Dedicated to my Dad and Edie who will always have a special place in our hearts.

Playground

to

Patrol

By Alan Oliver

Chapter 1 – The Early Years

I knew it would be grief as soon as I heard the front door bell ring. I had been out all day with a few friends round the flats. We found some old plastic disc things that we wrapped rubber bands around to make shields. What goes with shields, well swords and stones. My imagination as a kid was amazing. Swords made from old sticks and there always seemed to be stones and rocks around every corner. It wasn't me I promise. That typical one liner when someone is guilty of something but on this occasion, it really wasn't me. My mate Stuart had decided to start a stone war right in the middle of the road, right by my house. At the time it didn't bother me, it didn't bother any of us. We were playing and not causing any trouble until....Smash!!!. what my mate thought was a mud bomb was actually half a house brick covered with soggy mud. At the time I thought that was good until I noticed the damage. The wing mirror of a car was completely broken off and glass everywhere. Well, I was off, quicker than a missile.

"Who is this calling at this hour"? my mum said as she opened the front door. I was standing right behind her when the door fully opened. There he was, a giant of a man with a moustache as dark as the night sky. "Evening" he said taking one step into the hallway. I remember my mum looking up and standing back right on my foot. There was no point saying ouch because there was something more severe coming my way. It was a policeman, and a very big one at that. I thought for a minute I was having an out of body experience. Funny thing is, although I was really scared, I was more worried about my dad finding out. The policeman, wearing his tunic and beat helmet proceeded to tell my mum that someone's car had been damaged by a group of lads throwing stones in the street.

"It wasn't me mum" I said trying not to cry. I could see my mums face turning from that loving warm glow to a pale stern look. I knew I was well and truly up the river without a paddle. This situation couldn't be avoided. Would I get the slipper or the back of a hand? I was in trouble badly and it was definitely going to get worse. My mum looked at me a gave me the parental countdown option of coughing up within five seconds or my dad will find out. I knew that he would find out anyway and it was an attempt to soften the inevitable. "Stuart". One name, one answer. There it was. I blurted it out quicker than I could think it. I was only about 8 years old and didn't understand the concept of being a grass.

I could breathe easier, well slightly better than panting like a dog anyway. I knew this wasn't over. I knew Stuart would have complete deniability and this policeman would be back at my door again once he had spoken to him. The situation was unbearable and I couldn't keep in my tears much longer. I turned into a blubbering wreck, bubbles coming out my nose and red cheeks, no one understood what I was saying, then he said it. "well, on this occasion the owner doesn't want anything to happen as, he was very understanding, so I will leave it as that" he said. That was my first experience of dealing with the police and from that moment on I appreciated that this could have been a lot worse. He said he was going to see Stuart's parents too and a couple of others. Stuarts mum was worse than my dad, and I knew I wouldn't be seeing him for a few months.

He left me and my mum in the hallway. I was still crying uncontrollably hoping that my mum would eventually feel sorry for me. I was petrified for the next couple of hours until my dad got home and we were sitting at the dinner table. You could cut the atmosphere with a knife. "what's wrong doll?" my dad said. This was it I thought. Within the next few seconds I was going to be destroyed. "well I've had a visitor today" she said. Oh, mum just come out with it please and end this nightmare I thought. "the police came to the house today" she said. My dad stopped eating and put his knife and fork down. My mum began to explain the events until my dad stopped her mid flow. "I suggest you go to your room" he said looking at me. The look he gave me clearly making me aware that this wasn't over. I didn't even talk, slid my chair back and walked out of the room without finishing dinner. If I'm honest I didn't really start it.

Sitting in my room I could hear the faint voices of my parent's downstairs. I knew what they were discussing and what I could expect. I constantly reminded myself of the events of the day and how I wish I didn't go out and play but it was too late, what's done it done right? My bedroom door opened and it was my mum. A sigh of relief. My mum bought me a jam sandwich and told me I'm not allowed to come down for the rest of the night. She sat down with me and said that I had been through enough today and that my dad has said that he is disgusted that I had brought the police to our door. I understood and accepted my jam sandwich and words of advice with open arms. A kiss on the head as my mum stood up. "The only time I ever want police in this house is if you are one" she said. I knew what she was saying. I had disgraced the family home but never again, ever.

I towed the line for weeks. I even helped the couple move from next door. I was being a right little helper. Anything that I could do that would earn me 50p pocket money, weeding, helping my dad down the garage. I used to love it when he had sand delivered as it was perfect for my soldiers and tanks. I would spend hours down the back carving out little tunnels and ramps and had endless battles keeping myself for company. My dad didn't mind. He used to laugh it off when mixing the sand and cement discovering plastic soldiers in his mix. I thought I wanted to be a soldier when I got older. My dad wanted me to be a fireman and my mum just wanted to me to go to work wearing a suit and be her little Richard Gere in American Gigolo.

"What's your name?" I asked the boy standing outside the neighbour's house. "Jack" he replied. "I'm James" I said. This was my new neighbour. Jack's mum and dad came out. His dad, dressed in white shirt and black trousers. I noticed he had little holders on his shirt and flappy things on his shoulders. "hello I'm Jack's dad" as he held out his hand. "my dad is a policeman" Jack said. I had a few seconds of worry and a flash back of that day weeks ago. I had a policeman living next door to me. "I try not to tell too many people but I have just finished work" he said.

I ran back inside and told my mum and dad. "we've got a policeman next door". My mum looked at me like something was instantly wrong. "He's our new neighbour and they've got a son my age". I was really happy. There was a new edition to our group. There was no more messing about now especially if Jack's dad is a policeman. For the days and weeks ahead we spent hours together, playing outside, playing soldiers in the sand and the odd day trip with my mum. "Hi James, if you ask your parents, and if they agree, I'm taking Jack to my police club at the weekend and you are more than welcome to come". Well I said yes straight away and ran in to ask my mum. "of course, you can love". She said. I was so excited.

I remember the day well. There was a special event on. There were police cars and bikes and police officers everywhere. I was even allowed to sit in the cars and play with the sirens. It was brilliant. Even watching the other kids play inside and watching the blue flashing lights waiting for my go again was breath taking. Everyone was so friendly, even the police officers that were working. I was trying on hats and helmets and even got handcuffed. I could hear the static crackling noise of their radios and wondered how they could understand what was being said. I couldn't wait to get home and tell mum and dad how amazing it was. I was going to tell them that when I get older I'm going to be a policeman and help people and catch the bad guys.

The years were passing me by and I became a fan of Chips and the Bill. I ordered virtually all of the police videos that were on the market and watched them over and over. Looking back now it may seem a bit geeky but I really wanted to do it but I was still at School.

In my last years at school I took options in drama and music? I haven't got a clue why. How this would help me to fight crime I don't know. Nevertheless, I took my exams and left school. What next, I thought? too soon for the police and I didn't fancy college. I thought I may as well start to earn a crust while my mates are still getting pocket money from the bank of mum and dad. "Why don't you be a postman" my sister said. Early morning starts, delivering letters in all weathers. My mum even took my paper round out because I didn't like doing it. They were offering a cadet scheme and I was an ideal candidate. I gave it a go and got in. A couple of weeks training then the trainer said that we will be starting at 6am! I have never seen 6am in my life, only when I was born.

It was proper graft. Heavy bags, six-day weeks and a building full of life at every hour. I was really quiet as I didn't have the confidence to come out of my shell. I always remember my first week's salary,

£99.12. I was a millionaire I thought. I didn't understand the concept of planning and saving so I went straight out a bought myself a pair of trainers for £65. I was still quid's in, even having £24 left. I suppose being the quiet one helped me out a bit as I was asked to help a local school out representing the company working with several agencies and……. the police. The aim of the scheme was to promote safety in the community. A good idea I thought helping the younger generation. It was a week at a local community sports arena.

I went along and was given the task of answering a pretend 999 call and I was the operator. The kids called and asked for an emergency service and I signed them off if they done it right. There was a policeman there, on another exercise testing the kids about strangers. It was the last day when he asked for my help as his colleague was off for the day. "wear this" he said as he handed me a hi visibility jacket with epaulettes. It even had police on the back and front. I couldn't help but keep looking down and seeing the shiny silver numbers and letters. It was at that moment that I thought, I will never give up, I'm going to be a policeman and that's final.

I stuck it out for a few more years and eventually done quite well, but my heart wasn't in it. I would do my job well and would never go sick but I always kept saying that this time next year I would be a copper. A few of my mates even started calling me PC Plum and coppers nark. I didn't mind, I'm sure I will get called a lot worse I thought.

Chapter 2 – There's nothing to lose

The day had arrived. So, in order to calm my nerves, I thought I would buy myself some menthol chewing gum to take my mind off of the drive to my assessment. Chewing frantically to focus my mind on anything other than trying to pass the police recruitment test. The next episode in my adventure as I arrived near the assessment centre was to trying to find a parking space in time for 8am. The time was now 6.30am! My mind was distracted yet again, as everywhere I looked all I could see was where the recruits live for their residential training. My nerves were beginning to get the better of me when all of a sudden, my stomach started to churn over like all my worst nightmares were coming together at once. I needed the toilet more urgently than I needed life itself.

It was now 7am and I managed to find a space. 1 hour to go and now all I could think of was trying not to soil my pants and completely mess up, literally. It was decision time. Drive off looking for somewhere to go or try and get in an hour early despite the letter telling me not to turn up before my allotted time. Sod it, I will go in I thought. Walking up to the gates everyone else must have thought I had a dodgy leg as I was trying my very best to hold my bum cheeks together to prevent what could only be described as a major incident from occurring.

Morning, the security bloke said, have you got your pass. I nervously produced my letter saying that I had my assessment today. You're a bit early he said looking at me like I had just burgled his house on Christmas eve. Sorry, but I really need the toilet. I thought what else can I say, I'm keen, the train was early or more to the point, let me in because I'm just about to poo myself. Having blagged my way in I headed towards the main Hall frantically looking for a toilet sign. Well, it was like winning the lottery when I saw one.

There were a few people milling about, looking at my unfamiliar face. I was praying that no one asked who I was as I was at the point of no return within seconds. I really hope the toilets are empty because this will not sound too good. As I entered my eyes scanned the room like a hawk. Amazing feeling as I entered the cubicle, my belly was on fire, I couldn't get my belt undone quick enough. Devastating yet profound relief….

So, I had the toilet to myself, I began asking myself why my stomach instantly turned so bad. I've been nervous before but never been like this. Yeah, I want the job but still it didn't really explain why it felt like I had eaten 10 vindaloos, So I looked at the packet of chewing gum, well one of the three that I had been chewing for the last hour and a half. Do not consume an excessive amount as they will produce laxative effects. Laxative effects I thought, crikey…. I had a very lucky escape.

7.45am I walked back out to the waiting area where I saw quite a few other people, looking petrified at what awaits them. Very light conversation along with the occasional know it all who knew absolutely everything about joining the police, he knew who everyone was and that his future was already in the bag. A bit of an idiot if you ask me as he swiftly alienated himself from the rest of the group. The door opened and a very stern looking sergeant walked over. No hello, no welcome, nothing just a, follow me. Well this didn't help as I felt another twinge in the bowls. Too late now I thought I've got to just get on with it.

We were all given a quick speech about what to expect and told the normal stuff about calling the officers 'staff or sir and nothing else. You may begin the test he said. Not off to a good start because I even messed up on spelling my own name! How many squares here, and how many stars there, was the general gist of it and before I knew it we were all told to put our pencils down. My first reaction was that I well and truly messed it up. The relief was nice, although the stress began waiting for the results. Waiting patiently for what seemed like an hour I noticed there were about 30 of us.

The happy looking 'staff' reappeared holding a cup of coffee and called out quite a few names. It wasn't me and I never saw these people again. The know it all bloke wasn't one of them. He was quick to tell everyone that they had all failed and we were the lucky ones. Mr know it all eased my mind, although I wasn't going to allow myself to be so naive albeit he was right. Congratulations, you have all passed the entry test staff said. Next on the agenda is your physical and medical but that won't be until tomorrow as we have several pieces of admin to do and show you to your room for the night.

Everyone had to collect their belongings, the lucky ones, the others didn't even get the opportunity to unzip their bags. We all followed staff to the other side of the site. It seemed like miles but I felt a sense of belonging, a feeling of achievement. I was following a couple of experienced officers talking about a skid pan circuit down the road and that they had their advanced driving course tomorrow. That's sounds brilliant I thought, I want some of that I thought. The reality hit home again as we approached the residential block.

As I entered I saw some recruits walking down the corridor, smartly dressed in their crisply pressed uniforms. Morning staff one of them said as staff pulled him up about his boots not being shiny enough. Bloody hell I thought, he looked smart enough I remember thinking. His boots were proper clean. Staff got the keys from an old bloke whose job it seemed was to sit in a little office responsible for the running of site. I always remember my room, 13th block, room 13. Bloody hell I thought it this a sign?

As I walked in and the door closed behind me staff told me to meet downstairs in 30 minutes. My room, well if you can call it that, was equipped with a desk and chair and a bed with itchy looking blankets. Oh, not forgetting the sink, stainless steel all in one unit. A wardrobe with two hangers. That's it, nothing else apart from the noise of the wind circulating throughout my floor to keep me company.

I unpacked a few belongings and had nothing better to do than go back downstairs only to be met by everyone else. The looks on their faces, no doubt the same as mine that they just wanted this to end. The chit chat was still very basic, names were beginning to flow, what people work as etc. Staff reappeared, is everyone here? I think so someone said.

I will show you the shop while we are here staff said. It was like a little market, basic survival bits like soap, washing powder sweets and equipment that you could put on your utility belt, handcuff keys, pouches and torches there was loads there. No doubt they were making a killing as it was the only place to buy anything to survive. It was good though, I was eyeing up things that I would get if I was lucky enough to get through this.

Right, let's go and get some lunch staff said. I didn't think we would get fed and I started panicking slightly as I had the best part of £1.50 in my pocket so started sweating in-case we had to pay and I would end up with a packet of crisp and a tea and everyone else was tucking into something wholesome. As I walked into the canteen I noticed that there must have been 100 beat helmets on hooks, the floor, stacked on top of each other. How the hell do they remember who's is who's I thought but they did.

The smell of something roast dinner like seemed to be on the menu, which if I'm honest, did smell quite pleasant. As I followed the rest of the sheep into the canteen the noise of the already established recruits hit me. It seemed like they were all staring directly at me! Just tell the lady you are on your assessment staff said, it's free. That's a result I thought…I glanced at the food, it looked good, something with rice. I got my tray and joined the line. Sweet and sour chicken balls with rice and a sauce. A sponge pudding and orange or lemon juice at the very end. Not bad at all until I bit into my succulent chicken ball. I thought I misread the sign. My first bite seemed extra chewy, really chewy in fact so much so that I had to discreetly get it out of my mouth. I think the others thought I had a nervous twitch or something as my eyes were squinting like I just sucked a lemon. It was at that point that I noticed it wasn't chicken but pork and a bloody grisly bit at that. I then got stuck into the rice half thinking if it was actually rice and not something else. I was quite lucky with the sauce, they must have like me as I had two pieces of pineapple in mine as well as a bit of celery.

Who was I to moan. I mean free grub and I'm not even in the job yet. Grub over and we were off over to the medical block. We all sat in the waiting area, looking at each other thinking what does this entail. I knew an eyesight test would be part of it but then some lady came out and told us to put these on, hospital robes. What the heck do I want one of those for I thought. I'm glad my mouth didn't engage like my brain did otherwise I wouldn't last long. Into another room, robe on a back out into the waiting area.

My name was called. I stood up like it was a role call and was told to go into another room. As I walked in I was met by a couple of people, I assumed someone from the job and a nurse. Hello, I said in a very curious tone. I got a hello back so it put me at ease a little and took my mind away from a big box which was directly in front of me. OK, so if you can take your robe off and stand on the box for me please one of them said. My immediate thought was, are you serious, stand on this box with my meat and two veg on display. I wanted to say no but my robe came off without a second thought.

So, there was me, standing on this box, completely naked, in front of two strangers but what was I to know. Can you bend over for me please one of them said. I am seriously starting to ask what I have walked into here, no clothes, bending over. This was to make sure that my back was straight. Well I knew mine was, although as soon as I bent over it sounded like a set of fire crackers going off. I doesn't normally do that I said defensively.

What! the next test was a drop and cough. Cup my testicles and cough to make sure there are no issues. Well the cold hands didn't help but this went fine too. Everything was going ok considering I thought I was going in for an eyesight test. Thank you very much they both said as I left the room still wondering what had just happened. Oh, I forgot to say the eyesight test went fine too.

So that was that for the day it seemed. How wrong was I. Staff reappeared and told us to make our own way back to our rooms and get our swimming kit and not to hang about. It was getting on a bit now about 3pm. Keen not to disappoint the know it all bloke started running back to towards the rooms and for some unknown reason we all started to follow suit! Nonetheless the turnaround was about 10 minutes and we were all back by the pool.

There was another officer waiting for us by the pool, tracksuit bottoms and t-shirt. He didn't look very approachable and told us all to get changed sharpish. My first opinion of him was that he loved himself more than his other half if he had one. However, he was in charge not me. Changed into my swimming shorts we all waited by the pool edge. The over powering smell of chlorine lingered in the air. We had to swim up and down several times and pick a rubber brick up from the bottom a couple of times. This demonstrated that we could all pick a rubber brick up in a pool if ever required to do so in an emergency.

Right he said. Go and have a shower and wait for staff outside where you first arrived. That was it, nothing else, nothing further from this bloke, the end. The showers were communal and I didn't think I could get my tackle out twice in one day in front of strangers. I tried taking my time getting in the shower and considered keeping my shorts on. I just bit my bottom lip and whipped my shorts off and walked into the shower. Oh, for heaven's sake it was full up with blokes showering after their PE lesson. On occasion, and we've all done it, your eyes glance over to ensure that you are correctly displaying a reasonable package in comparison to boost your confidence. Well all I can say is this, the freak circus must have been in town because I may have well not had anything. How gifted they were. I gave myself the quickest wash down in history and shot out of there and got changed. I really hope I never see them again.

Staff was waiting as expected. We were all told, with our hair half dry and swimming stuff rammed into our bags to go and get dinner from where we had lunch. I will meet you there he said, just queue up like you did earlier. I wasn't really hungry, I only had grisly pork ball and rice a couple of hours earlier. I was starting to miss home already and I had only been here a day.

The canteen was a lot quieter when we arrived. I assumed that the other recruits were still having their classes. Apparently, they do an early and late shift for training so it was nice not to be leered at like we were being hunted as prey. The smell was still the same as earlier, that warm roast dinner like smell that you only get in schools and prisons. Shepard's pie was on the menu this time although it looked like a bowl of mince once the ladle had been scooped into it several times. Presentation was not being looked at so who cared. My plate was filled with the mince, a little crusty potato and some beans. Not bad at all this time round and I actually quite enjoyed it.

Staff joined us and told that once we had eaten to wait in the lobby area so he could show us around a bit more before we retired to our lonely rooms. This is the bar he said as we walked into quite a big room looking out onto some portacabins. The smell was exactly the same as a normal pub, the stale smell of alcohol, that one tone carpet that's easy to cover up fag burns and vomit. You can use this facility while your here he said although there are rules. You're alright I thought, I just want to go to my room and get this day over with.

I casually made my way back to my room with a few others, the know It all bloke was still going on about how good he was, and that he had already got the job as he knew people in certain places. I wasn't really paying much attention, just reading the signs on the notice boards about ironing services and where to get your hair cut. Block 13, room 13…. unbelievable.

Looking out of my window over world the realisation of having to spend weeks here hit home. Could I do it, what if I don't get on with anyone, what if I fail. This soon came to an end as the howling sound of the wind rushed through my room again. My window may have well been open as the draft that was coming through it was freezing! I thought I would find where the showers were ready for the morning. The stories I have heard from mates telling me to never wash in the sink in the rooms as they were used as toilets made me think twice.

Walking through the endless amount of creaky fire doors I found a brown door that said 'showers'. Walking in the smell of soap and deodorant hit me. Everything was tiled, everything. My first thought was that this could do with a makeover as I don't think it had ever been touched since being built. Nonetheless they were on my floor and not too far away. As I walked out I saw a recruit, alright mate he said, they weren't working today, there was no hot water in this block so we had to use the showers in the female block. Ah cheers mate, I said nervously. Where the hell is the female block I thought, how do I deal with this? The do not use sink option was looking the more viable option at this point. I wasn't confident enough to go walking around the place with my towel, shaving kit and clothes.

Back to my room I thought I would just get into bed and try to sleep this off. Perhaps a nice dream could take my mind away from the events of tomorrow. I think it's the physical. I knew I would be OK with this as I had been training for months and months, running in the rain with bin liners over me, press ups, sit ups, weights. You name it I done it. If anything, I was quite proud how I changed my body from being a little fatty to someone who had abs.

6am the alarm on my very primitive phone went off. Greeted by the moaning noise of the wind and some idiot shouting in the corridor 'the showers are out again'! oh for god sake I thought as I looked at the sink. I hope no one ever used it for a number two? I dragged myself out of the itchy blankets and turned the lowest watt light bulb on in the room. I had 2 hours before I had to be anywhere so I wasn't under too much pressure.... yet.

Turning the tap on my first thought was having a shave with cold water in a sink that you would never shine a UV light over. God, it was awful. I thought the water would have been fixed by now, I mean this is the police after all, right? Shaving done, my face looking like I had been sun bathing for 10 hours in the Sahara with no lotion and itching like I had fleas/ I thought I would have a quick flannel wash and shower properly after the physical as long as the freak show circus aren't in there putting me to shame.

Tracksuit on and down to the shop to be met by staff again. There was only me and another bloke there at bang on 8am. To say he wasn't pleased was an understatement. 8.15am the last person arrived and I could see that his name was clearly marked. Be there on time I thought, it's not difficult. You had to travel a couple of floors so why are you late? I heard that a few of them went to the bar for a couple of sherbets last night and didn't leave until 11:30pm. Not a good move when you're doing a physical in a few hours I thought but it's down to them.

Breakfast first, staff said. Back to canteen. I'm eating very light as I knew we would definitely get a beasting. Cornflakes and a gritty tasting orange juice sorted me out. A few others were having a fry up with teas and coffees. The canteen smells never changed regardless of what was being cooked it seemed. Right, we were off to the gym. We were met by the happy chap from the day before although today he had another bloke with him who looked even worse. I heard the know it all bloke saying that he was a professional rugby player and will beat everyone on the bleep test. He never shut up, I only wish I was as great as he was, not.

We were given a brief insight into what was expected by the two approachable instructors. A certain amount of press ups and sit ups required in under a minute, a standing jump, grip test and bleep test. Not too sad I thought, achievable. The bleep test was first. Beep, and I'm off. Start of level 1, then 2 and so on. People were dropping out at the 5, 6 and 7 marks. I kept going, 8 and 9. Know it all, as I have crowned him, was still with me. 10,11…. still going. We were the only 2 left now. The instructors were clearly happy with our performance. 12, I could see that lick arse wasn't happy that I was still with him. The rest of the group were now jeering us on. It felt good until the instructor said OK that's enough. He didn't win, he drew with me, the chubby boy a year ago. I could have kept going he said, panting and sweating like he had been chased by a dog. This bloke is unreal I thought. Thing is he was so desperate to win the satisfaction was all mine. I could see that the others loved it too! Well done me……

OK, quick shower everyone then make your way back to the room in the main block. That's where we all met yesterday and I had a menthol chewing gum issue. We were all waiting for staff to arrive which he never did. A woman appeared and asked us all to go into the room and someone will be along shortly. Those invited back for an interview tomorrow are as follows.... first name, then the second and third then fourth. This isn't looking too good I thought. Sixth then seventh then, like a tonne of bricks was lifted off my chest my name was called. There was about 20 of us in that room and eight of us got through. Everyone seemed to do OK but where they went wrong I will never know. Rareton Police Station at 9am tomorrow was my last instruction then I left with a passing goodbye and good luck from, I assume, the Human Resources lady.

Instantly I felt like I hadn't slept for a week and just wanted to curl up in a ball and close my eyes but I had the best part of a 2-hour car journey to get back to normality. Who should I call first I thought. There were no hands free then or loud speaker, I don't even think it was an offence to use your phone while driving but I could be wrong. I called my mum and told her the good news. She was like the BT hub for the family so by telling her the news would quickly circulate and circulate very fast.

I remember having a long shower, not worrying about the next phase. I ordered some Chinese food from the top of the road and after consuming that started planning my route using my now prehistoric desktop computer on a dial up connection. It took bloody ages because every time someone called the connection dropped out! This would be an early start again, alarm for 6am, train, tube then bus followed by a ten-minute walk.

Arriving at a massive police station I remember walking into the front office and seeing a couple of familiar faces from the last couple of days. Still looking scared. One of them was looking at notes, pages and pages of them. What can he be revising I thought, none of us knew what was going to happen. All I knew was that I was getting a burning feeling again in the stomach region and I did not want a repeat episode of the first day.

The door to the side of the front desk opened and a very official looking sergeant asked who was here for their interview. Yes sir, someone said. I'm not a sir I'm a sergeant was his response. He's failed before he's had his interview I thought, poor bloke. Walking up several flights of stairs the smell of oldness surrounded me. The building was dated. Pictures on the wall from even older times and trophy cabinets seemed to litter the beginning of every corridor. Old polished wood bannisters and tiled floors led into floor after floor.

Into a little waiting area with a couple of doors directly in front of the chairs. A dirty looking window and a few pictures on the wall that you would never consider buying yourself. My name was called first. Not long to wait at all I thought. Looking well turned out in my double-breasted pin striped suite and my brothers tie I walked into the room. An inspector and a sergeant awaited me. Take a seat young man the inspector said.

As I sat down the standard interview protocols were offered, taking your jacket off, water on the table. Right, so you want to be a police officer, do you? why? Said the sergeant. Oh my god I thought, a complete mind fart. The most predictable question and I didn't have a clue how to answer it. The milliseconds seemed like hours. Think,

think, come on you silly sod answer this easy question. Err well, I have always wanted to be a policeman I said. That's the best I came with. I could answer the question in my sleep now and answer it well. I've messed up and fallen at the first hurdle I thought and the interview demons had started to appear.

So, you get called to a domestic incident and the couple have been married for years and have children. What advice would you give them? asked the inspector. What advice I can give them I repeated over and over in my head. I would ask them what happened I said, and make a decision based on their replies. OK, said the sergeant, they don't want to talk to you now because you are very young and they feel that you're not in a position to help them and they ask you to leave, now what. My answer.... I would tell them I am the police and I am here to investigate a disturbance and would stay there until it was resolved I replied.

The inspector leant forward, and I always remember what he said. Look, you have done very well to get to this stage, better than hundreds of others and you are what we are looking for but you are too young. Go and get some life experience and come back in a few years. I know you are disappointed by this but I am sure you agree that we need officers that have a few years of life behind them. I was 18 at the time and agreed with what the inspector told me however gutted I was. Go and join the special constabulary for a bit and get a bit more experience that way. Do specials not deal with domestics then or wear the uniform I wanted to say. I was upset, angry and had this overwhelming sense of failure.

So, thanks for applying the sergeant said we will see you in a few years' time. That's it I thought, game over. 12 months of applications, 3 days of stress and for what, nothing. Little did I know that this would be the end of the beginning.

Chapter 3 – I'm doing this for the love

So, you want to be a special constable, do you? I would love to I said. This was a divisional officer I spoke to who was the equivalent of an Inspector in the special's world. He had phoned me up at home and asked me to pop down to my local station for a chat, not an interview, just a chat. Straight away I was already relaxed. This was about two weeks after my rejection from the regulars. I knew where everything was and drove down and parked outside. I waited in the front office and special constable came to meet me. Hello mate he said, a really friendly face bloke. I'll just sort you out a pass then I will bring you through.

As I followed this officer we walked down the stairs which I assumed was the basement area. We past the dispatch room where they despatched the calls. It all seemed very interesting. As we walked into a biggish corridor in the basement the first thing that struck me was how clean it was. Better than my last experience. This seemed modern and well kept. If you just wait there mate the inspector will see you in a minute. I was wearing smart plain clothes, not casual but well turned out nonetheless.

Hello, would you like to come in the Inspector said. A very old looking chap, very smartly dressed in identical uniform to a regular inspector. Take a seat…...So thanks for coming along tonight he said, I just need to ask you a few questions and do some admin if that's ok.. I've heard that you didn't get into the regulars and this is a solid stepping stone to get you there. Can you tell me what one of the biggest issues is in your area at the moment? I knew this straight away as three of my mates had their cars broken into along with mine so I said vehicle crime. That's perfect he said. Would you be able to commit around ten hours a week to being a special? Yes, probably more I replied.

There was a bit more chit chat about what goes on and the times people attend but at the end of the hour he told me that he would love to have me on board. I was shell shocked, overwhelmed, excited, ecstatic. He said I got the job, albeit voluntary, but I didn't care. I remember thinking that my police career starts here! You should hear from us within the next week or so James. The course is around 20 weekends either Saturday or Sunday and will be held at the college. A firm handshake and I was shown out by the same officer that welcomed me. I floated out if I'm honest.

It arrived, police logo on the front. I opened it frantically where I was met with the welcomed words, congratulations on being excepted into the special constabulary. You are required to attend The Police Training Facility on the date below. It was a couple of weeks away. I was so made up the time flew by. The two-hour drive didn't faze me one bit now as I knew that I was getting something back and at the end of it I could give something back. So, I got there at 9am as instructed. Hardly anyone about, I assume because it was the weekend. I had to wait in the same waiting area as I did about a month ago but this time without having the urge to soil my pants.

I was joined by about ten other men and women, a few had been in the same boat as me. It was still quite frustrating though as our commitment shone through as we all decided to turn up and would have made good coppers but the chosen route for us was this, so we stuck with it. The instructors were volunteers too. A divisional officer came to greet us and introduced himself and what was expected of us over the coming weeks and months.

You will be called upon to perform the role of a police officer. Your roles and responsibilities will be exactly the same. The public and the people you go to help and arrest will not know that you are doing this voluntary. They see a police uniform, not who is wearing it. They call for help and the police arrive and it will be you. Sound words I thought. Words that hit home. You will all be sworn in as special constables and swear an oath to the queen to uphold her peace and police this society without fear or favour.

We were lead into the main hall where we were met by an even more senior officer, the equivalent to a commander I believe. We were sworn in, we took the oath. The feeling was quite strange, I had put myself forward and had now been entrusted to perform this role. Congratulations the chief said, well done, you will now embark on an adventure that will stay with you for the rest of your life.

We had a cup of coffee and were introduced to our instructors. Again, a couple of volunteer officers that gave up their time to teach us the basics of policing. We were sat in a room with a direct view over the countryside.

So, welcome everyone. Let's start off by doing some introductions but I want it done with a bit of flare. If you have a skill or talent then introduce yourself using your skill or talent. Skill or talent I thought, I haven't got any bloody skills or talent that I know of. The first bloke said he could play spoons so some spoons were produced and the bloke introduced himself while playing spoons. The next was a woman who said she could sing, so she sang and introduced herself. Then it was me, the talentless bloke who was just about to make a complete idiot of himself. What could I do? I said I don't have anything, really, I don't. The instructor asked if anyone else didn't have anything and the rest of the class slowly began to put their hands up!

OK he said, I want all of you to think of a song and introduce yourselves while singing this song and I will be back in 15 minutes.

Was this a test, a confidence thing god knows, but I knew we had to do it. We all gathered round and some woman said we should do a rap. A bloody rap I thought are you serious? A couple of others said that's a brilliant idea. Really, I thought, is this police work? Anyway, outspoken and willing to participate we went with a rap. Boom, boom, shake the room. That was the one we went with if you remember it.

The instructors walked back in and asked if we were done. Yes, staff I said. OK, let's hear it then. All I can say is this. It was the most embarrassing, rubbish rendition of that song I have ever heard, although working together we done it, job done. Well done the instructors said, very good. I couldn't help but think that they were taking the mick out of us.

It broke the ice, got people laughing and involved. If I'm honest it was quite a good approach to bring us together. If your all going to be police officers then you will all need a uniform. We have got the uniform stores open today so you can all get measured up and issued your kit. Wow, I thought, I am actually getting a police uniform.

This is getting very real very fast. Off I went, following a few others, everyone desperately trying to outpace each other so they could be first in line but without being noticed. It was a short walk, behind the swimming pool where I became a qualified rubber brick rescuer. That experience all seemed so distant, but it led me here, still working towards my goal of doing this job for a career.

It was a proper set up. Changing rooms, mirrors and loads of uniform hanging up. I forget where I was in line but I heard a few people saying that their size wasn't in so they would have to wait. In I went, an old boy with a tape measure around his neck. He didn't ask my sizes he just went to work measuring me and guessing. He done my waist and said 32. 34 I replied. No, you're 32 so its 32. bloody hell even the uniform bloke has got attitude. OK, I said knowing too well that they would be super tight and look like they have been sprayed on. I'm not going to argue with the bloke because I've only been here a few hours. Right, try that all on he said.

This was it, wearing the cloth as its referred as. When I say I had to breath in to do my trousers up was an understatement. I had to wrench them over the plastic white shirt they gave me and then do the belt up. The belt was meant to be leather but it was like a strip of steel. The shirt instantly made me sweat as it had a thick cardboard like strip down the front. This cloth was not designed for comfort. I squeezed it on, struggling to breath but too afraid to say anything. Then he pulled a jumper out of a plastic bag and said try this one. As soon as I touched it my fingers started itching. What is this made from I thought, the same stuff as the blankets in my room. Without asking I stood in front of the mirror and a police officer looked back at me. It was me, but policeman me. I looked the part although I didn't feel it. It was very uncomfortable.

Take it all off now he said, you're not having those, those are our try on items. Oh, so when do we get it then asked. In about ten weeks he said. Ten weeks! that's bloody ages away I thought but I'm not going to say anything. I'm at that stage that if they asked me to clean their shoes I would. You know what I mean if you've been there. You are keen to impress, don't question anything, do what they ask you to do. I put my civilian clothes back on, said thank you and walked back out into the waiting room where the next person was waiting to walk out with their uniform today.

Sitting with the others the general talk seemed to be where and when we collected our warrant cards. Some bloke who looked about twelve years old knew so much about the subject you thought he made the bloody things. It seemed like these warrant cards were like the holy grail. The waves would part if you ever had cause to produce it. I had no urgency to get one but listening to what they were saying it did seem pretty exciting. One of the instructors appeared and the 12-year-old asked when we would get them. At the end of your training he said. We never issue them too early because there's so much training that needs to be done first and we want to make sure you can do that before we give you it he said.

You could see the disappointment on a few of their faces, and mine a little. Looking back now we all wanted everything straight away. Giving you the tools to do your job without knowing how to do your job seemed pretty stupid when you think about it so now I understand the reasons why. Someone asks for help and you whip out the holy grail and haven't got a clue what to do next. As soon as I get mine I am scribbling out the special constabulary bit so it looks like a regular warrant card the child looking bloke said. Oh, here we go I thought, we haven't even got our first day out the way yet and he's already talking about how he's going to be super cop.

The last person was done and we were lead back to our classroom. We were told to challenge anyone who didn't have a pass or was in plain clothes on the site staff said. Well that's all of us I thought as we met that criteria as we haven't been issued nothing yet. It seems that we were being drip fed little bits of responsibility to boost our confidence or challenge us I don't know. I felt like a wild animal ready to pounce at a second's notice. They were turning us into police officers. The sense of belonging I felt a few weeks ago was rushing back. I really want this I thought, and want it badly.

We were given a tour around the main building and shown where the classes would be held. There will always be a dress of the day staff said and this will be on display here, pointing to a glass cabinet and the bottom of some stairs. You will need to nominate someone to let the rest of you know what to wear. Today's dress I noticed, was jumper order and beat helmets. You will only walk in pairs around the site and walk correctly staff said. Walk correctly I thought, one leg in front of the other, I had that sussed out when I was about 2 years old.

You will have drill at the beginning of every training day by the drill instructor that you will meet shortly. This is to get you ready for your passing out parade. Now that seemed like something I wanted to be a part of. We were lead out into the parade squire, well car park, but for this exercise it was a parade square. Standing there, a sergeant major type character, shiny wooden cane and no eyes. The peak on his hat was literally covering his eye balls! Right, he said, stand on the yellow line, come on come on he shouted.

When I say, I want you to give me your best march up to the other yellow line, turn around and march back. I've got this I thought. We were all numbered off, I was number 5 I think. The first girl marched off like she was dancing, the second bloke like he was shadow boxing, the third and fourth were fine then it was me. Off I marched to the yellow line, turned and marched back. Have you been in the military he said. No staff I replied. I thought he was impressed until he said. I didn't think so. Oh, I thought I must be bad.

Nevertheless, everyone else done it, a few were awful, some were funny and some were very good. Whatever the case maybe we all needed some help with this otherwise the passing out parade would look like a drunken lunatic's convention.

My first day was coming to an end. A mixture of excitement and exhaustion surrounded the parade square car park. Back up to the class room staff said. All sitting down and telling each other how bad our marching was I couldn't help but notice separate wads of paper on the corner table. I assumed they were for another class. These are all yours the staff said handing out the bundles to each of us. This is your basic reading material to learn when you are not here. Within this lot are your basic definitions, theft, robbery, criminal damage, your bread and butter policing material. It was a good few inches thick. You will be tested on this next week! Next week I thought, this would take me a year. I normally go out most evenings after work. If I'm going to do this then my lifestyle will have to change.

Leaving the site and beginning my long drive home I began to look at things in a different perspective. People seemed more suspicious, shiftier and I noticed a lot more than I normally would. Am I developing the renowned coppers nose? I felt tired but couldn't wait to come back next week. I thought I would give myself the night off and start the studying tomorrow night after work.

Work finished and the piles of paper were looking at me asking to be read. Here goes nothing I thought. I was never a keen reader at the best of times and got an F in English at school because I simply didn't have the time for it. Theft. A person commits theft if they dishonestly appropriate property from another with the intention of permanently depriving the other of it. What the hell does it mean by that? It has to be tangible. What did it mean by that? Oh, for god sake this is like reading gibberish I thought. I skimmed through it and moved onto robbery, still with a theft element but confused the heck out of me. Criminal damage, well, what can I say. It confused me more than the other two. How the hell am I going to remember all this stuff let alone be given a test on it. I had to devise a strategy and devise one fast. The post-it notes came out and I began breaking stuff down, vital elements and repapered my bedroom wall with legislation. I ordered a hypnosis CD, tried meditation in order to stimulate my brain. The hypnotherapy CD arrived on the Wednesday and I plugged myself in and tried to get hypnotised. The bloke sounded like a dirty caller, telling me to walk up towards a cottage in the mountains where all my fears and foes were. He told me to go into a room where I had the only key and conquer my fears. Conquer my fears I thought, this is utter nonsense. 3,2,1 you are now awake he said! Now bearing in mind this pile of junk just cost me £25 my only regret was being 25 quid out of pocket. I never did get hypnotised, unless I'm still under hypnosis now.

Friday arrived, like the whole week was only 24 hours long. Was I feeling confident, no. was I nervous? yes. My biggest concern was making an idiot out of myself and getting 10%. Saturday arrived and I arrived early. It was good to see everyone. One person never showed up and must have thought it wasn't for them. It was only a 30-question exam, desks in exam conditions and the rules were laid out. If we cheated we were out, honesty and integrity and all that. Right, OK, put your pencils down please staff said. It seemed like a minute.

It was ages and a hellish wait but staff came back with the results in hand. Congratulations everyone he said, you all passed. One of the girls asked what she got. Well done I thought, publicly humiliate everyone why don't you. He gave hers first, 80%. good score with the pass mark being 70%. he got to me 86%. A few seconds to absorb my glory then I responded with a smile. There was only one person that got 96% so I did feel a sense of achievement. Not bad from someone that could spell FUDGE with their exam results. Keep this up staff said and you'll be out on supervised patrol in ten weeks or so. I found out that your uniform should be here within a few weeks so not as long as expected he said. Supervised patrol, what go out on patrol I thought. I couldn't wish the weeks away fast enough.

The weeks did go by, a few more exams, a few role plays and some more drill practice. Learning the caution was interesting. You do not have to say anything....it took quite a few attempts but once I straightened out my tongue it was alright. The passing out parade was within touching distance and it felt like I was on the home run. It was actually eleven weeks when our uniform arrived, much later than planned and not three weeks, but nonetheless it arrived. It was all there wrapped up like a big Christmas present minus the glitter and bow.

Now you have got it you got to wear it staff said. We all slipped off to our respective corners a whipped our civilian clothes off quicker than a drunk on a promise. I remember those trousers now and that shirt with the designer cardboard strip down the front. It went on, quite tight but it went on. The moment had arrived. The beat helmet of justice. We didn't try it on at the initial fitting as they had none in so it was done by measurement only. You would have thought it was the coronation all over. It was on, itchy jumper as well. I looked at my reflection in the glass and although not perfect that copper was looking back at me again. I looked down and side to side to admire my uniform.

Looking up I saw my class mates. The room was full of coppers. Most people would panic walking into this room but for me, us, it was family, the police family. Right then, staff said. You all look the part now let's get on with it. Let's head over to the main parade ground and start rehearsing the passing out parade. This is getting better by the minute I thought as we walked in pairs, sort of marching, over to the parade square. The drill instructor was waiting, very smart and military looking as usual. We knew what he wanted from us now so he wasn't that scary. Get into line he said, measure off then number off. A few shuffles high to short we were looking like a proper outfit.

All of a sudden, brass band music started to blast out of speakers around the square. Our orders were giving by the left, quick march. Every step-in line with the beat of the drum, arms shoulder high, head straight and desperately not wanting to mess it up. I was actually marching around the parade square as a copper. Halt, 1-2-3 stop. Perfect I thought, just perfect. I want it exactly like that staff said. We wanted it like that, it looked good, it looked professional.

After an hour or so we went back to class. Staff told us where we would be going and to get our shoulder numbers for our epaulettes. I got mine and began struggling with the little metal clips that never fit on the pointy bit. They were on, I was fully equipped apart from the truncheon and handcuffs. No sooner did I think it they appeared. You have got to sign for these staff said. This is your truncheon and your handcuffs. Well, my pen couldn't come out fast enough. Signed, received with thanks. I was complete. You are allowed to bring your kit to your respective stations but must bring it back for next week. There's no need to bring your truncheon back staff said.

A few of the others had already arranged when to go out at their stations, not me. I phoned up the equivalent of a sergeant at my station to arrange a date. Please say Friday, please say Friday I thought. What about this Friday 7pm, is that alright with you or is that too soon. Too soon, no chance. That's fine I said, I will be there at 7pm. Staff asked if everyone had arranged something and I was glad to say that I had.

Friday 6.30pm. As I walked up to the front office where I was a few months earlier, police cars were shooting out of the back gate. Blue lights flashing, sirens going clearly going to something juicy. Another officer met me and walked me down the same stairs to the basement. This is your locker room mate. Pop all your gear in there. We have got parade in 5 minutes. OK I said, not knowing what he was on about. I followed him like a lost puppy as we walked into a large room with old fabric chairs. There were around ten officers, all specials, all very welcoming saying hello and how are you.

Parade, someone shouted. Everyone stood up. What the hell is going on here I thought? It was the inspector. Apparently, we all stand when a senior officer walked into the room. Please sit he said. He offered me a warm welcome and asked me to introduce myself to the team. No skills or talent required this time just my name, what stage of training I was at and where I lived. The inspector asked the sergeant to give the postings which meant who is working with who for the night. They even gave call-signs for cars. Cars I thought, I thought we walked everywhere.

My shoulder number was called along with another. I looked around and couldn't see anyone with that number. Panicking slightly, I felt a hand on my shoulder. Hello mate, you'll be with me tonight. He was a big fella although he reminded me of a teddy bear I'm Steve. I latched onto him like a new born baby. There were a million questions I wanted to ask but I was as keen as mustard to get out and about. I knew the area very well and was half thinking that I would bump into my mates and end up nicking one of them. Arresting someone was a scary thought, I didn't know what to do. I knew the cautioned but that's all. One step at a time I thought, slow and steady.

Steve showed me the radio room and how to turn the radio on and what channel to use. He explained the correct way to talk to the control room using the phonetic alphabet. God, I hope I remember it I thought A is for Apple, B is for Bert I think? Right mate, we have got to look the same so I suggest jumpers and coat tonight. We will have a walk around the town centre and see what's what. All I ask of you is that if things go wrong you call for help and know where we are he said. What was he expecting to happen, are we going into something bad, do I need to let my mum know? I now understand that if the it hits the fan and you need help then get the troops running, you can cancel them later.

Our shoulder numbers were written on the board in the control room and we headed towards the front desk door. As Steve opened it I could see a few people in the waiting area. They all looked directly at me. They didn't know I knew bugger all, they saw was a policeman and wanted me to expedite their waiting time. I didn't make eye contact as I couldn't handle any questions. I was new, nervous and if I'm honest terrified.

Trying not to breathe out too much and pop the clip on my trousers I found myself holding my stomach in which after a while gave me belly ache. Walking up the main road I could see that the town centre was busy. Cars and people everywhere. One of the biggest nightclubs had a queue to the corner a good 300 yards or so. I knew it would be busy on a Friday night as I'm the one who is normally out in it, getting drunk and making a nuisance of myself. Things were different now, I swore to uphold the queen's peace. I was the police, it was me and the family that would keep these people safe tonight.

Go ahead over, I heard Steve say. I didn't even hear the radio, something I must learn to do but it was all a bit alien to me. We have got reports of a disturbance in Bronze Street. The door staff have ejected someone and he's threatening to stab them. Are you sure about this I thought, how would we deal with this? We were about half a mile away so we broke into a little trot. My god, trying to run in my skin-tight trousers was a mission. The cardboard shirt I was wearing was rubbing on my chest and my massive radio was smacking against my bum all while trying to hold my helmet on. It must have looked funny to see but for me it was awful.

Show us on scene Steve said. Received, update when you can please as we have other units making way the control room said. There were loads of drunk people hanging about and the smell of stale alcohol filled the air. It seemed that everyone was smoking too. I always remember some drunk bloke trying to light his fag the wrong way around and was asking me for a light. Sorry mate, I don't smoke I said. He asked me about ten times. I wanted to tell him to bugger off but I had to remain professional.

The door staff, all giants with skin heads and tattoos said some bloke was harassing some girls so was asked to leave. He had taken a brave pill and wanted to fight us but he's gone now. Phew, I thought, that was handy. God knows what he was drinking, these blokes were enormous and would have completely destroyed him. I still had the drunk smoker by me. I need a light he said again. Look mate I said, I haven't got one now go away. The aggressive I'm hard side of the drunk came out. You're all the same you pigs, all the same, all I want is a light. This has gone up a level now, the list of offences I had learnt, well three of them, were racking through my brain. Well he didn't fit into any of them unless he stole something or damaged something. Steve came over. Right, you've got 3 seconds to go away or you're getting nicked for drunk and disorderly. 1, 2 then like Steve had a magic wand the drunk turned and staggered off down the street.

Good skills I thought. Don't get distracted by idiots like that mate. Be stern with them, if they don't go away and are causing a noisy nuisance then arrest them. We can't have aggressive drunks walking our streets. Our streets…. I always remember that. We were the sheriffs. OK, Steve said can you give them a result. Who I thought? When you call up use your shoulder number and tell them what happened. It was only talking on a radio so why did I feel that I was giving a speech at conference. I had to do it. My thumb edging towards the transmit button. Control 1312 receiving over. I sounded like a robot on crack. Go ahead. The result for man threatening to stab people is….is…. Steve, uttered male made off before police arrival, advice given to door staff. I repeated that word for word. That's all received thanks. I had done it, spoken on a police radio. It was really like the Bill.

We were now in the heart of the town centre. Drunken activity was rife, hundreds of them. The occasional office worker making their way home but mainly party goers. There were door staff on every pub, club, wine bar and even a few restaurants. A good sign or bad I don't know. All the door staff nodded as we walked by like they were our back up. They really help us out sometimes Steve said. When it gets really busy we could be on our own so we need their help. But we are the police I thought, there's an endless supply of us if it goes wrong surely. So, Steve, how often does it go wrong then I asked him? Most Friday and Saturdays, the ground is very big. Not only is there the town centre to patrol but all the other calls, domestics, disturbances, suspects on he said. What's a suspect on I asked. Oh, that's when there is a suspect on someone's premises like a break in. It would take time to learn the lingo but it'll come I'm sure.

1312 receiving, 1312 are you receiving? Oh, that's me. I gave my robotic go ahead over. Are you anywhere near the market, we have reports of youths smoking cannabis by the amusements. Steve nodded. Yes, show us dealing. Received. Job number two within 20 minutes. It was only around the corner but I knew a shortcut through some old shops. We were there within a minute, no running required this time so I arrived without panting and sweating. Can you show us on scene I said on the radio? There were dozens of people hanging about. It was dark and quiet in the market. The smell of the old fruit and a few static carts remained in the street. The lighting was poor. I never ventured down here myself as it was a bit of no go area known for trouble. I had never smelt cannabis before. The smell would remain so distinctive and frequent throughout my career. Then it hit me. It smelt horrible. Why people would want to stink like that beats me but each to their own I suppose. There was no one there smoking this garbage. I updated the control room with the result.

Steve said it's a common problem. People phone in but there's a delay through the system and by the time it gets to us it could be ten minutes old. A lot can happen in ten minutes mate. Let's have a walk in the car parks he said. Walking in the stairwells which smelt of old urine and disinfectant Steve asked me if anyone had shown me how to use my truncheon yet. I wanted to crack a crude joke but didn't know him well enough. Right, hold it like this, strap round here and you're ready. If it breaks you can use the butt. Well I said, I hope I never have to use it let alone using it after its broken. You never know mate. I haven't used mine in four years he said.

We better get you back now as you've got training tomorrow. I felt more relaxed walking back having been out for a few hours than when I first walked out. As it was getting later I could hear other jobs over the radio, fights, officers calling for assistance. They were all miles away from where we were and we didn't have car. Do you drive Steve? I said. Yes mate, we are out in a car next week. Really, the immature little boy in me said. Yeah, so try and get in for 6pm if you can.

Back at the station Steve rubbed our names off the board as we were back safe and sound. The inspector asked me how it was. Really good sir, I learnt a lot. That's good he said. Kit away in my locker. See you next week Steve. Yeah, take care mate you done really well tonight he said. I done well I thought as I left holding my head high. Walking out the front office door where I first arrived with no one paying me any attention this time.

I was posted to a response car, I was in the station van, I was in the drunk patrol minibus. Everyone was trying to better each other the following morning. I didn't want to get involved with all that. We all had a good experience, well except one bloke. They put me in the front office he said and I done nothing for a few hours. They wanted the regular officer out on the streets so they replaced him with me he said. I was sussing my class mates out now. There were a couple that could talk for England. If you had a big car they had a bigger one. I made an arrest last night one girl said. Staff asked what for? An assault staff. Good work staff said, can you talk us through it. Well the look on her face was one of terror. Err ummm well I was with the officer who made the arrest and I put them in the van. Oh, staff said so you didn't arrest them? No, I did. Where she was going with this story I don't know. She was crowned the class blah merchant. Staff didn't dig any further clearly thinking the same as me. Let her have her moment I thought, it makes her feel better.

The following Friday arrived and I turned up at 5.30pm. I knew the code to the door now so could let myself in albeit I didn't have my warrant card yet just my little visitors pass. Alright Steve I said.

Hello James, I've got us a car. Bring your flat cap and hi—viz as you may need it. I got my little kit bag that contained some note paper and waterproofs and we walked up to the yard. Sitting there was a mini metro, single blue light. This is ours Steve said. Just chuck your stuff in the boot. As I opened the boot a ballistic vest was in there, first aid kit and a fire extinguisher. I really wanted to wear that ballistic vest because it looked good but it was covered in dirt and dust as it never saw the light of day.

Sitting in the car there was no technology just a single button that said blue. We had a different call-sign tonight, a vehicle call-sign. We could get to loads more calls. Steve had only just started the car when we were being called. Group of youths causing a disturbance the control room said. Roaring up to the gates and waiting for them to open Steve pressed the blue button. It wasn't a turbo charger to boost our one litre engine it was to activate the little light on the roof. I remember looking at the reflection in the houses seeing the blue light flashing, it was amazing. Cars were pulling out of our way as Steve was pressing the horn. This thing didn't have a siren just a beep beep beep. It wasn't the fastest car. We even got overtaken by a riot van going to the same job! We got there and believe it or not there was a group of kids hanging around outside a chip shop. There's was about six of us and ten of them. They were all cocky and gobby. I couldn't help but think that if I spoke to a copper like that my parents would smack my back side hard! This is LOB Steve said. LOB is that another code I thought? What's that mean Steve I said? Load Of Bollocks he said. I got told to jot down a few names and then that was it. They were given a telling off by one of the regular officers then they walked away with their tails between their legs.

Any available unit, large fight in progress outside a nightclub a few miles away. Show us I said. The radio was my new best friend. We shot off again, beeping down the road arriving on scene within a few minutes or so. There was indeed a fight going on, well loads of pushing and shoving and handbags at dawn as they say. There were a few other units there. This was a time when people genuinely got worried when the old bill turned up. Drink had got the better of a few of them and they didn't heed any advice. Right, he needs nicking Steve told me, drunk and disorderly. Well this bloke was about 6ft 5 with the brightest ginger hair I ever did see. This would be my first ever arrest and I couldn't mess it up. Sir, I am arresting you for being drunk and disorderly. The caution flowed nicely. Then I realised that I had to handcuff him. I had my foot-long radio in one hand and pocket book in the other. Why I had that out I don't know. I couldn't clip my radio on my belt so ended up putting it on the floor! On the floor, it makes me cringe thinking I done that but nevertheless I handcuffed him and put him in the back of a van. No cage in these and there was room for the other two too.

When they were in the van staring at the three coppers that had arrested them one of them noticed that they were all ginger! Under arrest or not this bloke could have been a comedian. He was a funny guy and it removed any hostility that there was throughout the trip back to the station. Steve was with me. I could see that he was even cracking a grin at this bloke. Arriving at the station all three were taken out still very jolly. Is my room ready one of them said? I asked Steve how we were going to get the car back. One of the regulars have taken it now. This will keep us busy for a couple of hours he said.

Next, I heard a voice coming from within inside the custody block. As I walked in for the first time, a tiny custody suite presented itself. Behind the desk was the biggest sergeant ever. Big red face, buttons on his shirt looking like they were about to explode off. So young man, why have you brought this chap into my custody suite. Offence, time of arrest and time you arrived here will be sufficient he said. Err Drunk and Disorderly, 22:10, 22:30 sergeant. So, you have been making a nuisance of yourself after having a few too many have you son the sergeant said. Yeah, the bloke replied. The sergeant went through a few legal bits and another copper took him to a cell. That was it, first arrest, booked in and now standing around not knowing what to do next. Luckily Steve was next so I just waited for him. Once Steve was done we went to the canteen. It was 24 hours then. I got the teas and we sat down and started writing our notes of arrest. These won't be too long he said. Start off with day, date time and place and that you were with me. Steve was right, these notes, handwritten took about 15 minutes to knock out. There's not much to say really, we got the call, turned up, they were drunk and being loud, they got nicked he said. Fair enough I thought……. the night came to an end and I went home with a feeling of achievement. I'm getting there, slowly but I think I'm doing alright. I did think as I curled up into my bed how the bloke I nicked is in his cell. Is he regretting his actions or did he just go to sleep I'll never know.

There wasn't much chit chat the following morning especially from the girl that said she made her first arrest last week when she didn't. Staff was saying that we should concentrate on a couple of exams that we've got coming up and more rehearsals for the passing out parade. We were nearly there and the remaining weeks flew by. I hadn't been on patrol since my arrest. There was no point me going on patrol and failing my exams. A couple of role play tests and two written exams were done. We all passed. Well one bloke had to re-sit a role play but he got through still. We were given our warrant cards, the holy grail, and given a very stern talking to about misusing them. It was more than getting kicked out so it went firmly in my back pocket where it stayed.

Next week is your passing out parade staff said. I have some white gloves for you here but I must have them back for the next class.

Today we had a full-dress rehearsal. Tunics, white gloves, polished boots and medals. One of the blokes was ex-military and was draped in medals. I was slightly jealous because I had nothing but I was passing out so I didn't care. There were a few senior people at the parade square today and the brass band that would be there on the day. They weren't dressed in their gear but were there just to play. It really was a moving moment. After we done a near perfect rehearsal staff told us that it was an early finish. Make sure your uniform is crisp and clean and your boots polished he said.

I was nervous and a little sad that my training was over. Will I see anyone again, who knows. I was the only person who went to my district. On the morning of the passing out I forgot my white gloves. Talk about getting myself in a state. I remember running over to the main bloke where a Saturday lady was working and begged her to loan me a pair of white gloves. At that point I owed her my life as she produced a pair from her draw.

Lined up with other officers from the other classes the band was at the front. In front of the band were police horses, fully dressed in ceremonial gear. The drill instructor was at the side looking crisp. Claaaaas class attention. You could hear a pin drop. I could faintly hear passing traffic and the occasional cough from the spectators and other officers watching the parade. This was it, the moment I had worked hard for, the conclusion to the beginning. The band started playing. Class by the left in three's quick march. We were off. It sounded magical and from where I was we looked the part. As I turned the corner entering the parade square I saw my mum and dad sitting there watching. It brings tears to my eyes writing this as my dad was my inspiration, he passed away a few years ago and I love and miss him so much.

I could see the satisfaction on their faces, my dad giving me a thumb's up as I marched past. We went around the square once and came to a halt in front of the parade box where the senior officers were. There was a speech by a Deputy Assistant Commissioner about what we had achieved and thanked us for our contribution. We saluted the officer and a few seconds after marched back round the square to where we first started. That was it, job done. Stand easy, class dismissed the drill instructor said.

I made my way around the corner to where my parents were. Well done mate, my dad said as he offered me a firm handshake with his rough builder's hand and a hug and kiss from my mum. It meant so much and I can still feel that kiss and handshake to this day.

Chapter 4 – Let's give it another go

So how is your maths? the female sergeant said. Not bad I replied. If you get through the maths test you're going to be fine. The college was beginning to feel like my second home. I was here again, applying for the regulars. No one could ever say that I gave up. I gave the specials as much time as I could but it was voluntary after all. I got promoted at my full-time job which meant that I couldn't commit to the hours any more. I still had this passion within me to be all I could be and being a police officer was that missing link. The maths test was similar to the one years ago but I passed it. The entire process was different. It wasn't crammed into three days it was split up which if I'm honest made it better.

The letter arrived. Congratulations you have been successful in your recent application for the role of police officer. Further joining instructions will follow once a course date has been allocated to you. I was on cloud nine. It had taken me the best part of two years waiting, phoning, emailing asking when my assessments would be. I just hope that it's not going to be another two years before I start. It wasn't, it was about two weeks before I got my next letter. Your start date will be in October. We were in July. I had to get things rolling and resign from my current role as I didn't know what the time scales were.

The day had arrived and I had experience unemployment for a few weeks. I came prepared and brought a sleeping bag to lay on top of those itchy blankets. I guarantee that they were still there. My mum and dad came with me and saw me off. Good luck they both said. I could see they were even more proud now as I was doing this for a living. I walked in the gates along with a few others. I didn't recognise anyone. Everyone looked petrified. For some it was all new. At least I had been there before and knew my way around. Everyone gathered under the main block. There were a few recruits already a few weeks ahead helping us and telling us where to go next. I was told to leave my belongings and head towards the canteen. An orderly queue began to form and I could see a couple of uniforms sitting at a desk in front of me. It was two sergeants I noticed. Hello what's your name and have you got your letter.

Handing it over and giving my name, I still didn't know what to expect. The number I am about to give you will stay with you throughout your service and you may want to write this down he said. Thank god, I had a pen, many didn't. I had my warrant number, I had a status, I had a purpose.

I was ushered away back to my belongings to wait for everyone else to finish. There were dozens of us. The process of getting a room seemed more regimented. Name, room number, keys. Back downstairs in the canteen in 15 minutes. You can sort your stuff out later. Ironically, I was in the 13th block again but not room 13. Everything was exactly the same. There had been no makeover. I could see a big housing development being built from my window. The howling wind was still making an appearance and my window wasn't breezy although it was a nice sunny day so it was too early to tell if I needed to wear my coat in bed. The itchy blankets were still there but I wouldn't be sleeping on them because I came prepared.

Back outside a few other blokes were waiting by the lifts too. Alright lads, I'm James. I'm Paul, Dave and Simon they said. I had broken the ice with hopefully some new mates. Secured with a handshake we all headed back to the canteen. I'm really nervous Dave said, me too said Paul. Simon just nodded in agreement. As the lift doors opened we made our way to the canteen. It was only a short walk. I couldn't help but notice that the posters for haircuts and ironing services were still there. They looked like the same ones! Nothing ever changes here I thought. It serves a purpose to train new officers like a conveyor belt. Strangely enough Simon piped up. It's not exactly a five-star hotel is it lads. Not really mate I said.

Walking into the canteen we all nervously sat down. A few recruits lingering about eyeing up the fresh meat. The two sergeants standing at the front both holding cups of coffee. That roast dinner smell filled the air that hadn't changed over the years. The chitter chatter between everyone just sounded like a moaning noise which came to an end very quickly as an Inspector walked into the room.

New recruits, please stand for the Inspector the sergeant said. I have been here before so knew what was coming. I was half minded to stand anyway but didn't want to be the odd one out. All standing the

Inspector invited us to sit again. Welcome to the police training college. Some of you will spend the next however many weeks of your life working, eating, sleeping and studying very hard to become police officers. It isn't easy but it's achievable. The weeks will pass very quickly he said. I was thinking about the 'some of you' bit that he said? Then…. Some of you will be moving to another site miles away. We have opened another training site where some of you will be trained there. You will spend a few weeks here carrying out your officer safety training and first aid and a few other bits and then you'll be off. It's not far.

OK I thought, another base would be perfect. Five weeks here I could handle. Weeks and Weeks could be a bit of a struggle. Please listen carefully for your names as this will be where your training will take place. The names began to flow, Here, New site, New site, Here…. the list went on. I heard about this new site. It was easier and I could drive so the travelling would be bliss. I was praying that I would be sent there. My name was called, New site. Brilliant I thought. Five weeks then I'm off.

This process complete, we were all lead back to the main hall. Dave, Simon, Paul and myself were sticking together. We were all posted to the same place which was good news. I think we are getting sworn in I said. The main hall was a grand place. The smell of history surrounded it. Really old paintings on the walls of high ranking officers and a bigger one of Her Majesty the Queen. The oath was the same, full of strength and commitment. We all said it together which gave it more power. Congratulations and welcome to the service the Inspector said. You are all now police officers, subject to you passing your training. Can I just thank you all for what your about to undertake he said?

One of the sergeants took over and told us that there was a bit of paperwork that we had to do and asked us all to collect various pink, blue and white forms from the side and fill them in. Next of kin, insurances etc. That complete we were split up into our respective classes. There was about twelve of us that were going to the new site so my class was quite small in comparison to others. Everyone in my class looked quite normal. No one came across as the teacher's pet type. We were just, well, normal. We were lead to a class room back over by the canteen. Pictures still the same, the dress of the day cabinet was still there. We all sat down, the room was very cold and sounded hollow. These were my classmates; my colleagues and I was keen to get to know them. An officer walked in, E on his epaulettes. Good morning, he said. Just like school we all said good morning staff.

He asked us to introduce ourselves so he knew something about us. There was a chef, artist, post office staff, mechanic you name it. It was a right mixed bag. No one from any legal or police back ground whatsoever. He handed out pens and paper and asked us to write down a short biography about ourselves so he could read them at his leisure. Mine was a few pages long, nothing too glamorous.

Right today he said, we will get your uniform and get your photos done for your warrant cards. This was moving faster than when I was doing the specials. Over to the uniform block where we all waited patiently to be called. It was a good opportunity to have a chat with my new pals. As I went in the uniform bloke said hello. Again, nothing had changed. A quick look up and down, a measure here and there. Try this on he said. The jumper had changed and wasn't made of that itchy rash causing material. Uniform on I looked in the mirror. It was that copper looking back at me again. This time round I stared. This is what people will see when they call for my help.

Is that all OK he said? If you want an extra size up now is the time to tell me. A bit different from last time when it was a case of get what your given. You can put it all in here he said. An enormous black holdall. We got absolutely everything. Shirts, trousers, ties, belts, jumpers, helmets, flat caps, batons and handcuffs. This was exciting. I wanted to keep it on but couldn't. This took a bit of time because we all got more kit. If you drop this back to your rooms and go for lunch be back at 1pm for your warrant card photo's staff said.

Lunch, sod that I thought, I'm going to the shop to get my inspector gadget bits for my kit belt. It was like the shop knew we were all coming because they had stocked up good. Everyone had the same idea. The adrenalin kept our hunger at bay and the shop soon filled up like a January sale. Pouches, handcuff keys, torch holders it was all there and I got it all. I don't think anyone realised that I longed for this day my entire life and to buy these bits. I even bought a credit card wallet with the police crest on it, god knows why because I only had one card.

There was a about 20 minutes left so me and the boys darted round to the canteen. Chicken curry was on the menu or a strange looking salad. Funny though because it still smelt like a roast dinner again. A little further down the line in an area never frequented was a little fridge containing yogurts and those pots of rice. Caramel, banana or vanilla were my choices so I opted for the banana. The orange juice machine had a queue by it so I opted for coffee only to be presented with a machine I couldn't work. I didn't know where the hot water button was. I looked like a right idiot and felt people looking at me. There it is love, said one of the ladies that worked there.

Sitting down with my mates I proceeded to open my yogurt only for the silver tag to break off forcing me to use my teeth. Oh, for god sake I said as too much force caused it to spit banana yogurt on my shirt. Brilliant I thought. Warrant card photos with banana yogurt on me. A few people chuckled but not too openly as it was early days and no one really knew the true you at this stage. I sucked it up because I would have laughed too.

Back to the classroom and we were told to put our white shirt and black tie on with epaulettes. Our names were called to go into a little make shift room with a pale blue curtain. Do not smile, the bloke said, just sit down and look directly at the camera. 321 and it was done. Thank you he said can you send in the next one please. I thought we would get them straight away but was told it would be a few days as they normally prepared them at the Head Quarters.

He is ready for the next one staff I said. There were only a few of us left. That was the advantage I suppose of only having a few in the class. Dave was the last one to go in and while he was gone box after box was being brought into the room. I could see writing on the top but couldn't make out what it said. There must have been hundreds of boxes. The ones that blank A4 paper come when you order in bulk. Dave came back in and the staff said that in these boxes is your study material. A box each I thought so they must be for the entire intake. Every box is labelled with your name so spend some time sorting this out and getting it to your room. Dinner is at 17:00 and I will see you back in this classroom at 08:00 tomorrow.

That was it, day one over. I looked at the boxes and we all began to shuffle towards them. I found one that said James, then another and another and another. I had six boxes in total. Stacking one on top of another they reached my shoulders! What the hell is all this I thought. it's all full of paper and we have a limited number of weeks to read, digest, do exams, all based on police theory and practice not including PE days I thought. I had resigned from my previous job so there was no going back. I had to do this and do it well. Three trips it took me getting this back to my room. This was the first time I had really been on my own. My room full of so much stuff I could hardly move. Where do I start I thought? It took me a couple of hours to sort this mess out.

5pm I went to dinner. Bumped into the boys. Chilli with rice tonight with a naan bread? Must have been left from lunch I thought. The pudding was a Jam sponge with custard. Strange combination but I was hungry after only having a spitting yogurt for lunch. We discussed who was going to run down in the morning to see the dress of the day notice. We agreed to take it in turns with Paul doing it tomorrow. We all had a whinge about the amount of paperwork, what we all thought lay ahead and a general moan about the 5-star accommodation.

We headed back to our rooms in block 13. The wind had picked up now and was whistling through the corridor. My strategy was to shower last thing at night just in case the boilers were playing up. I'm not falling for this again I thought. As I entered my room I closed the door behind me and heard the closing of the latch echo in the corridor. I felt lonely, lost and afraid. I had years of protection from my parents and now I'm here. No one to call downstairs to, no one tell me it would be alright. I had to shake myself out of this otherwise I would be on anti-depressants before the nights out.

I decided to organise all this paper into week order. There was so much of it, some weeks thicker than others. Study notes they called them and they weren't wrong. There were 1000's of study notes that

I almost went snow blind. Just as I was coming to the end there was a knock on my door. It was Dave and Paul. Alright James they said. They were all dressed in their uniforms. Have I missed something I said? Na mate, we thought we would take some photo's in our gear. New class mates and all that Dave said. A nice touch and another brick built in the bridge of friendship I thought. Give me a couple of minutes and I'll be ready.

When I went out Simon was there too. Right where we doing this then? Dave said. Out the back was the general consensus. There we were, all standing there smartly dressed taking each other's photos to send home. We did look the part if I'm honest. We had a laugh and joke about how pretty we all looked. A few laughs and proper laughter too, not that pretend stuff, tears and everything. We had formed a bond in a day, a good bunch of blokes, they were my mates.

The showers worked that night and I didn't bother having a shave as it hardly showed. 6 am, alarm going off my first night was over. I took my time then waited for Paul to let me know what the dress of the day was. 7 am. Jumper order mate Paul said, meet by the lifts in ten he said. We all met by the lifts and went downstairs. It was a fry up, but if you didn't want that there was cereal. I opted for the fry up. I'm not normally one for eating a dinner for breakfast but it felt like I was always hungry. As we were finishing our grub staff appeared. Sorry, he said can you all get changed into your PE kit as you have got Officer safety until lunch he said. Can you all write your names on your white t-shirts down the left-hand side in black pen too he said.

Oh, for heaven's sake, I have just eaten a cooked breakfast and now I have PE. We all went back upstairs. White t-shirt out of the wardrobe I proceeded to right James down the left-hand side. Only one minor issue after I done it though. I forgot that it was being tucked in so when I put it on and tucked it into my shorts my name wasn't James but Jam. What a complete fool I thought but it's too late now. Meeting up again and feeling greasy and needing a poo we headed over to the gym. No sooner did we all arrive staff said we needed our kit belts and handcuffs. He really shouted at us to run back and get it in under five minutes or we will have a 5-mile run to welcome us back with.

I won't lie, I was tired, puffing and panting like I was on the run. I made it back just, along with everyone else. We were all red faced, sweating and breathing heavily. Right staff said. Over to the track, let's go, come on he said. Thank god it was only a few hundred yards away. OK, staff said, get your breath do some stretches. We are going to run this track five times, I think it was five. You are having a laugh I thought. I almost died running to get my kit belt. I was starting think that this was all staged and that they knew all along that we had PE and still let us fill our bellies up with sausages and bacon. My urgent desire to have a number two had past as my body was starting to experience trauma.

Line up on the start line he said. Let's go…. I started off with a pigeon step jog and so did the boys. The only way I am getting through this is at a steady pace. 2000 meters. I had reduced this to about 1800 when I started blowing out my backside. This was tough, tougher than I thought. Yeah, I did do some training but the run back to get my kit belt buggered me up. There were a few others dropping like flies after the first lap. This is pathetic staff was shouting. Keep it going or we will be doing this every day unless you pull your fingers out he shouted. My mates were still with me, struggling like me, but we were still trotting making progress. Half a lap to go, the end in sight and I really didn't feel well. My legs were like rubber. I had no control over them anymore. 200 meters, 100 meters, done. It was over, Dave, Paul and Simon didn't look too clever either. Paul couldn't even talk he was so knackered. Dave's face looked like it had been in a wind tunnel it was so red. We didn't finish last, it wasn't a competition anyway. Within five minutes or so everyone else had finished.

Well done for finishing staff said follow me. We all limped behind until we came to a halt on the grass area opposite the gym. So, has anyone heard of CS spray he asked? A few hands went up. It's what we use staff Simon said. Correct, it's little liquid crystals that react when they come into contact with water like your eyes. Staff was joined by another instructor holding two big fire extinguisher type things and two gas masks. You will experience the effects of CS gas as you may have to use it one day. Their masks went on. Stand in a line the muffled staff's voice said. They both went to separate ends of the line. Do not rub your face was the last thing I heard. The spraying begun on our chests. It did stink and I began to think that it didn't work. I saw a few others coughing and moaning then a few more. One of the girls looked like she was on her way out. Her face was bright red and it wasn't from the running. Snot was dribbling out of her nose like it was on tap. I must be one of the immune one's I thought. The staff gave me another squirt right on the chest again. Well, the feeling of glass being rubbed into my eyes overpowered me. The burning feeling combined with my nose exploding with snot. I was blind and in a load of discomfort. This stuff was hardcore. Open your eyes and look into the wind I heard staff say. Open my eyes, you are joking I thought. This is so painful I'm not even sure that they were allowed to do this. It was unbearable. It wasn't going away, if anything it was getting worse. After a few minutes I knew I had to attempt to open my eyes at some point. I could see watery daylight. The burning feeling and the overwhelming smell was easing. Second my second every little breeze was blissful, easing the discomfort. A few more minutes and

I could see again. It looked like zombie film. People still moaning, staggering about, dribbling profusely.

Right, go and wash it off staff said. Make sure you use warm water as it clears it up quicker. Well like a bunch of drunken lager louts we staggered over to the toilets. We couldn't have a shower because we had no towels so we all hunched over the line of sinks like Quasimodo. Warm water, yeah right, I thought. The splashing of the water was spreading the CS everywhere. It was like pouring a kettle of boiling hot water on my privates. Warm water irritates it even more. My bum crack was on fire, testicles burning, face like it had been sand blasted. This was really bad stuff. Thinking that I had just witnessed a breach of the Geneva convention I walked back outside to the laughter of both instructors. Yeah funny that I thought. That is CS gas staff said. Go and have a proper shower and be back in the class room for 12:00.

Me and the boys walked back, all looking like we had been subjected to an atomic blast. Showered, with cool water, and got dressed in our uniforms. I suffered, we suffered, for the rest of the day with the effects of that. I hope I never have to use it I thought. Little did I know….

So, did you enjoy that staff said as we were all sitting back in the class room. Yeah, really nice experience I thought. There were a few laughs behind the red faces. We began learning basic legislation again, theft, robbery, criminal damage. There was some stop and search stuff in there too. Before you go you will have to pass a few exams First Aid, Handcuff, Baton techniques and tactics and some role plays. If you don't pass you will be back classed and have to start from the beginning. This does happen because I have heard the rumours. Sod that I thought, there is no chance of that happening. Although I've known them for a few days I didn't want to lose my pals. I was going to work really hard.

Those few weeks went quickly and the exams and roleplays went without drama. Everyone passed over 70%. The really hard stuff starts when we get to the new site. My last day at the college arrived and I brought my car for the last day as I had to bring all my stuff home. I would never have to use that train line again to go home for the weekends, well for the moment anyway. It was a sad day leaving the site, such a historic place. The memories of thousands lingered in every building. I had joined those memories.

Monday morning, I left home and arrived in a side street near to my new training base. It took me about half an hour. This degree of travelling is fine I thought. Struggling to carry all my uniform and study notes I felt like a donkey. I saw a couple of other donkeys walking in my direction but none of us could talk. I saw Dave in the distance. It looked like he had moved house. He seemed to have double the amount of stuff I did. My pace naturally caught up with his. Dave, what the hell have you got I said. Everything, they told us to bring everything he said. Mate, not all your shirts and trousers. We are not staying here I told him. Aren't we? It was too late to drop his entire kit back to his car so he muscled through and we arrived at the gates.

Simon was there, no sign of Paul. A few others from the class were lingering outside too. Has anyone pressed the buzzer I said?

Everyone looked at me with blank looks on their faces. It was beginning to look like a charity shop outside. Bags upon bags of clothing and police equipment. I heard voices from behind the door. A big blue metal door, no windows, no key hole just a handle. It opened outwards and a head popped out. Morning, an officer in uniform said. You must be the new recruits he said with a smirk on his face. Gather your belongings and follow me he said.

It was quite dark on the other side. A car park and a little smoking area. It was all wet on the floor like the roof was failing to do its job. Across the yard I could see the building was a few floors high. The officer walked to another door, this time it had a window and was semi open like the door needed trimming slightly because it wouldn't close. Into the corridor and the smell of the base introduced itself. It seemed like all the police buildings I had been in all had the same aroma. There was a lift but there wasn't a hope in hells chance of using it with the amount of stuff we had. Luckily for you we are on the third floor the officer said.

We all made our way up, struggling and scraping out big bags on the walls leaving scuff marks we were lead into a classroom. Paul was already there along with the rest of the class. We were all back together again. Grab a seat and put your name on the card on the front of your desk. I will be your instructor the officer said. The college rules still apply and you are to call me staff. There will be no drill or marching here and you don't have to wear your ties. Bloody hell I thought how relaxed is this. This bloke came across as a proper geezer which made me feel even more relaxed, he looked approachable and caring.

You will all be going to Green District. We will sort your shoulder numbers out later today he said. A few minutes after a sergeant and inspector walked in. Class, Dave shouted and everyone stood up. Thank you they both said. The inspector, or governor as I've heard them being called, gave us the same chat that we had a few weeks back. He told us again that we will be off to Green District. There you will complete quite a few weeks where you will work with an experienced officer. Green district is a busy area he said, very diverse and has its share of crime. I remember driving through that area once, years ago with my Dad. I remember there was a big shopping area near the town centre and it looked rough as hell.

The weeks flew by here and there were a couple of casualties. My days were 7.30am till 8pm. Long days but I wanted to do well and pass. One bloke resigned and one got back classed because he failed an exam twice. A bit harsh I thought but I understand why they done it. Your passing out parade will be at the Sports and Social club staff said. In a way I wanted it to be at the college and so did a few of the others. It was such a prestige place and such a grand ceremony and we were going to have it down the road.

The day had arrived. We were going to pass out. Our new district shoulder numbers clearly displayed and our boots gleaming. They took me ages to polish but I had a little cheat on the day and used one of those sponges. Hanging around the yard at the station a few of the blokes were having a last-minute fag. It was a surreal moment. I had been waiting for this moment for years. I never thought in my wildest dreams that on this day, such a memorable day, that I would become a fully fletched copper. The coach arrived outside and we all walked into the street. The public were all looking, glaring at us and pointing. They didn't know where we were going or what we had achieved.

Arriving at the club we were met by all our friends and family. My mum and dad were there again on queue as requested. My dad wasn't well, he had been diagnosed with an inoperable brain tumour and his life was coming to an end. My heart was broken yet he was strong enough to be there, smartly dressed in his grey tweed jacket. His rough builders hand held out and I grasped it firmly. Well done mate he said well done. My mum gave me a cherished kiss and I said my goodbyes as we were asked to get ready. I will make them proud I thought, struggling with the lump in my throat and bottom lip shaking.

We were all in the main hall, sitting at the front and family behind. The Chief Officer for green district stood at the front in his powerful position of authority. The names of my class mates were starting to be called. Dave was first, he walked up and shook the hand of the chief. A quick photograph and back to his seat. A few others followed then it was me. This officer has passed out with a distinction, something which is very hard to achieve but he achieved it the chief said as I nervously walked up. I shook the hand of my future boss and he congratulated me for my achievement. I walked off forgetting my photo and had to be called back. I put this down to stage fright. Photo done I walked back glimpsing over at my parents. My dad looking on, still doing his best to focus I gave a little wave, a wave of love, joy and thanks, thanks for being my inspiration.

Once every one had got their certificates I remember Paul calling me smarty pants and that I would shoot through the ranks. Doubt it I said, I was lucky. I worked hard and it was tough. You get out what you put in was my driving quote. A few sandwiches and light conversation and we were dismissed and allowed home ready to start my new job next Monday morning.

Chapter 5 – I was a Bobby

I knew where it was, I knew where the front door was but parking was a different story. This was an active police station. I couldn't exactly walk into the front office with all my kit. I desperately needed to park close enough so I didn't have to relive the donkey moment from a few months ago. Then, as if someone heard my prayers a car pulled off right by the back gate. Shooting into this space like whippet I could semi relax. I noticed another door, dark blue with a keypad. As I began unloading my career from the boot I noticed someone come out. Hold on mate I said. Can I just prop that door open so I can get my kit in I asked? No worries this bloke said. Can I see your warrant card? It was the first real time that I showed it and with immediate acceptance he let me in.

Walking into the yard I still didn't know where to go. There were doors everywhere, left and right turns and outside stairs going to different buildings. I began walking slowly. Slowly enough that hopefully I would see another person to ask where I was meant to be. I walked past all the police cars, dozens of old pushbikes and mopeds and into an undercover area. I saw one of the girls from my class. Aright Jo I said, where have we got to go I asked? Apparently, we have all got wait here until the trainers arrive. Sliding my kit bag off my shoulder I began to suck up the reality of my new working environment. At a glance it seemed alright, the building was again dated and I could hear the occasional cheer coming from the canteen.

The others were all starting to arrive, Dave, Paul and Simon and the rest of the class. A couple of officers arrived, quite friendly faced blokes. Hello guys and girls, one said. One more slog and you can get rid of your kit and get changed. Through another old door we entered into a long corridor. That police station smell hit me straight away. I still don't know what it is even to this day. The old polished wood doors stood out and the tiled floors lead us up to the third floor. This room was massive. Computers littered the first half of the room and a conference table at the far end with a couple of offices.

We were told to sit down on the table. I started chatting with the boys. There seemed to be an air of confidence about us all now. Nothing like a when we first started months ago. Welcome to green district a sergeant said as he walked out of his office followed by another sergeant and the trainers. Green district is a very busy area he said, this is an excellent patch to start your policing career. You will find yourself presented with all types of incidents to deal with, some good, some bad. All types of incidents I thought, like what? What does he mean by bad too? Everyone respects the police, don't they? Everyone does as they are told surely? We are the police, the last line of defence. How wrong was I….

He started talking about himself, what he had done, what he had achieved, how good he was and why he got picked to train us. This went on longer than the introduction. I couldn't help but think he was blowing his trumpet slightly. This course is quite a few weeks long and you will all need to complete the elements within these binders. If you don't complete them then you will not go to a team. The binders didn't look very thick but I suppose I was used to inches of study notes every week. There are reports you need to write, jobs you need to attend and offences for which you will need to arrest people for he said. You will be allocated a trainer between two of you. Arresting people seemed daunting, taking away someone's liberty. I had to do it, that's why I was there, that's what I wanted. Right he said, the female locker rooms are there and the male locker rooms there. They are all named so go and get changed and meet back round the table in ten minutes.

We all scrambled to the lockers and found our names. Some were bigger than others. Poor Dave could just about hang his own clothes in his let alone anything else. Mine wasn't as bad but I still had to put my bag on top. The tops of these lockers have never been cleaned I thought, so dusty and dirty with the remnants of old historic kit littered along the top. A few sprays of deodorant from the boys and we had to vacate the room as we struggled to breathe.

Back round the table one of the trainers was handing out binders and pocket books. Put your names, shoulder numbers and station on the front of both. Keep your pocket book with you at all times. Never leave it lying about especially in the canteen as you may find a penis drawn in it or a pair of breasts the sergeant said. Believe me it happens and you will fall foul of a prank or two in this job he said. How right he was….

Listen out for your shoulder number as this is how you will be called from now on when on parade. Mine was called and part of me didn't want anyone else apart from Dave, Paul or Simon. I was with Paul thankfully. I could see the smile on his face and no doubt he could see mine. You will be with Pete. Pete looked like he could handle himself, about 6ft 6inches and very big and looked like he wouldn't take any crap from anyone.

This is what we are going to do today he said. I will show you around the station and then we will go for a walk into the town centre. There wasn't much to show around, a few rooms, the canteen and the report office where all the officers write their reports and the radio room to get our radios. This is the BONGO seat, pointing to the front office chair. What's that I asked curiously? We post an officer to the front desk every day, they **B**ook **O**n & **N**ever **G**o **O**ut…BONGO. We both chuckled to ourselves. No doubt there will many more elusive terms that present themselves over the years I thought. I won't be expecting much, but if a call does come out and we can deal with it we will he said. Bloody hell I thought, this is really happening and if I'm honest is a little scary.

I would never walk this distance nowadays but we began the long walk into the town centre. The trainer walked slightly behind so it didn't look over powering with three coppers huddled together. It felt strange, the looks we got from society were strange. Some looked welcoming, some looked hostile. I knew at this stage that everyone is not our friends. I was praying that we wouldn't get stopped or flagged down. My radio was constantly busy with calls being dispatched and general chit chat. For some reason Paul's radio was on maximum volume and could be heard from the other side of the road!

As we approached the town centre it was full of people going about their business. The roads were busy and the whole environment was noisy. Paul's radio didn't seem that loud anymore as the noise of the community was louder. The instructor joined us and told us to keep an eye on each other. Don't be afraid to talk to people he said. No one looked approachable and no one was approaching us. I had that feeling again where I was analysing everyone and everything.

Is that you Paul said? Is what me I replied. I think they are calling you on the radio. Really, go ahead I said. Can you attend the high street where there are reports an abusive male who is believed to be intoxicated the dispatcher said? The robotic voice came out, yes show me I replied. Our instructor approached me and said that this male could be in play for drunk and disorderly so I will be looking for an arrest if he is still there. An arrest? What me arrest someone I thought.

Paul and I made our way to the high street where I was hoping that this drunk bloke had walked off. How wrong was I. There he was, swearing and shouting, kicking bins and old cardboard boxes. There were dozens of people watching like it was entertainment. There were people videoing on their phones and a few people goading him on. Right, this is it I thought. I remember saying that this is my moment. Not only am I being assessed I am being judged by the community.

Hello mate I said in a soft tone. What do you lot want. Mate you need to calm down, we've been called here because you are causing a disturbance in a public place. The smell of stale alcohol lingered around his body and his clothes were dirty and wet. I would put him about 70 years old but still quite a thick set bloke. I could feel the clock ticking, my instructor looking at me to take action and to take it very soon before he stepped in. A few more attempts to calm this bloke failed and then I said those words again, but this time as a regular. I am arresting you for being drunk and disorderly in a public place. You are drunk and are being noisy and aggressive to passers-by. As I went to handcuff this bloke he began waving his arms about like he was on a fare ground ride. Paul stepped in and help me get the handcuffs on. The cautioned flowed like it had been rehearsed for months. Well done the instructor said as he called for a van to take this bloke to the police station. I had done it, arrested someone. Ok it wasn't crime of the century but it was a crime and I was the first to arrest someone and I had only been out half an hour.

I could hear the distant sound of sirens and within seconds the van arrived. This bloke was still shouting and trying to wave his handcuffed arms about. Don't forget to search him my instructor said. I wanted to say that there is no chance I am putting my hands in his pockets but I couldn't. I asked Paul to hold onto him while I put my medium sized rubber gloves on. They should have been large but the station didn't have any. As I placed my hand in his pocket all I could feel was cold and wetness. I started to pull out soggy tissue and what seemed like dozens of coins. He had about three lighters, none of which worked and a packet of fags that were soaked. The smell of alcohol was stronger as the contents of each pocket was disturbed. After questioning myself over and over if he still had anything on him I put him in the back of the van. I knew I had to jump in the van to watch him as we went to the police station but Paul and the instructor had to come too so it was a bit of a squeeze.

Arriving at the police station custody block the bloke had calmed down slightly and was becoming sleepier until…the van door opened and he filled the rear yard with abuse and drunken spray from his mouth. It was like we had woken the evil dead. Paul and myself lead him into the custody block and presented him to the custody sergeant. To say the bloke was uncooperative was an understatement. How the hell do I control this I thought? Right, the custody sergeant shouted, if you don't calm down you will be going straight to a cell. I wish this sergeant dealt with the bloke on the street as he listened to him and calmed him down instantly.

So why is his man here the sergeant said? I explained the offence, allegation time of arrest to the sergeant. Right give him another search and put him in cell 10. My medium sized rubber gloves were still on making my hands feel a little numb now. The dirt from this bloke's pockets had made them all brown. He was proper filthy. I didn't find anything else so I lead him into the corridor where cell ten was. Most of the cell doors were open with the exception of a few. I put him in the cell and walked back to the sergeant. Well, all I can say is this. The looks on everyone's faces when the bloke walked back out and asked for some water was one of horror. Did you not close the door my instructor said? Immediately I knew I was in the dog house. No, I replied. I started shaking, the fear of instant dismissal overwhelmed me. Oh mate, this is unbelievable. You don't put a prisoner in a cell and not close the door behind you my instructor said. The pathetic excuse of I didn't know wouldn't wash so I just held my hands up and said sorry. There was no other way around it. I was new, inexperienced and fragile. I knew that I had completely messed this up until the voice from behind the counter reassured me. We were all new once mate, just learn from this the sergeant said. That was it, a lesson learnt and page in history written.

It was quite easy back then. A few notes and the arrests were handed over to a specific team that done everything. We caught a bus back to the station. Not the best form of transport but I suppose crime doesn't just happen on the streets. I was the talk of the day, one arrest, one massive cock up but I was keen to keep it going. I was fortunate enough to get a tick a in my binder which was an achievement in itself as it was only day one. That was it for the first day and a day I will always remember for the right and wrong reasons.

Day two arrived and I knew the code to the back door and where I was going. I didn't have anything to carry so it was quite blissful just walking in. I sat at the table and waited for the days postings. The boys were there. Yesterday's nightmare was still joke of the day. The sergeant appeared. We are all going out in the mini bus today. It's important that you know the ground and know it well he said. We all met down in the yard with flat caps and Hi-Viz jackets hoping to go out in a riot van. I was quite taken back when a hire van pulled into the yard. No blue lights or sirens just stickers on the side about hiring this van for £49 a day. Nice touch I thought, undercover work so soon.

Clambering on I quickly discovered the BINGO seat. This was the seat right at the back. BINGO, **B**oll%cks **I**'m **N**ot **G**etting **O**ff. Good name I thought but not for me. I sat right by the door ready to pounce at a moment's notice. The sergeant sat in the front. This would be a recognised position for the sergeant throughout my career. A couple of instructors sat in the back with us. We drove about for a while, everything looked the same. There were several estates, alleyways and cul-de-sacs. Right the sergeant said. Your colleague has been injured, you are under attack by a violent crowd. There is a radio in the car and you need help quickly where are you he said are? The silence filled the minibus. Green district someone said. Ok, but where he said. The silence became uncomfortable. You could see that the sergeant was not a happy man. I cannot stress the importance of knowing where you are, your life or your mate's life could depend on it he said. As we drove out of this little cul-de-sac we were instructed to look at the road name. I will always remember it and have used the road several times over the years to educate others. Observation Close it was called. A very aptly named road I thought, very appropriate.

Can we have a unit please to attend a sudden death the dispatcher said? One of the instructors answered straight away. Yeah show us. OK who wants to deal with this? Well after what seemed like an eternity I offered. Well done mate it's only around the corner. I could feel my heart pulsating, hands beginning to sweat. Panic was starting to set in. I am actually going to see a dead person I thought. Questions were whizzing through my head at a rapid pace, what do I do? what shall I say if people are there? It was awful. Arriving outside the address it seemed like an ordinary house in an ordinary road. There was a further update other radio that it was a concerned neighbour that called police. The instructor and I were dropped off allowing the others to patrol the district. Right mate, the doors locked so what power are we going to use to get in if we don't get an answer he asked? I knew this, section 17 PACE I said, to save life and limb. A glance through the window showed the TV on and curtain semi closed. I couldn't see anything else. I knocked on the door and then rang on the bell a few times. My instructor shouted through the letterbox but nothing. No noise, no movement nothing.

I will show you how to force entry he said. He called up on the radio and told the control room of our intentions. The noise of the first boot on the door was like a building coming down. Whatever was on the other side had been knocked off causing something to smash. The second boot and then the third the door frame cracked and the door opened slightly. One more boot and it flew open. Standing on the door step I looked directly down the hallway into the kitchen. The stairs were to the right of me. There was nothing, no voices just the sound of an empty house.

It's the police my instructor said a few times. Right in you go he said. Creeping in I was half expecting someone to jump out at me. Half of me was scared half of me wanted to see this chap lying in bed asleep. Nothing in the front room, nothing in the dining room. The kitchen was clear. Walking up stair's I noticed the old carpet and pictures on the wall. This was an old person I thought. As I got to the top of the stairs I noticed the room to left of me, a bedroom with the door open. I could see feet from behind the door, lifeless, no socks just bare feet that looked purple. I took a deep breath and walked further and into the room. I've found him I said. As I walked into the room the lifeless body of an elderly man lay there. No movement, no sound just someone's dad or grandparent who had left this earth for a better place.

I didn't know whether to cry, be in shock or be a police officer. I had mixed emotions. Right mate, have a look about and see if there is anything suspicious about this and I will call the sergeant back down the instructor said. If you start making your notes you will need to record everything, times, names, medication he said. I was still in my state of mixed emotions but I knew that I had to do this not only for me but for this man's family and respect for him. I comforted myself by pretending that he was still with us but asleep. Strange I know, but it made me feel at ease. It seemed that he was on his way to bed and something happened and passed away just before his bed. There were no other injuries, no blood or anything just him, asleep on the floor.

I took it upon myself to cover this gentlemen with his duvet cover. I wasn't allowed to move him. Pete said that I had to search the body to make sure there wasn't any hidden injuries. I didn't want to and I think he could see that. Are you alright he said? Yeah, I'll just put my gloves on and I'll do it. Gloves on I touched the cold lifeless body of this old man. I could see the front of him so gently rolled him onto his side to have a look at his back. His whole body moved in one turn as rigamortis had settled in. Everything stayed where it was. I didn't see anything. As I rolled him back I heard a gasp, a breath, an effort to come back to life. It scared me and I was stunned. Its OK mate Pete said, it's just old air escaping as he hasn't moved for a while. I was silent, speechless and I couldn't bring myself to move. I had never experienced that before and I never wanted to again.

I heard over the radio that the sergeant was heading back to us but there had been another sudden death about a mile away and Dave was dealing with that one. I wanted to call him, to prepare him, to warn him about what to expect but I couldn't. I was scribbling down everything that I had done along with times until the sergeant arrived. This doesn't look suspicious he said. You can jack up the coroner and try to find next of kin details. He didn't hang about as he had to go to Dave's one which was apparently worse. Right then, Pete said. Have a look around and see if we can find a name for this chap and hopefully a relative. I felt uncomfortable looking through his belongings but I needed to find out who he was so I could tell his family. I found a few bills and a bus pass confirming who he was. I found some other bits with his daughter's address. Pete contacted the control room to arrange for an officer to go and break the bad news. I'm so glad it wasn't me.

A few hours later a couple of smartly dressed chaps arrived from a local funeral home to take this gentlemen on his last journey. That was it I thought, found by me, looked after by me and seen on his way by me. It was quite an emotional moment. Pete had a look at the door and it worked fine. We would sometimes call out a boarding up service to repair doors or windows if they are damaged badly. You can never leave a building insecure he said.

Standing in the front garden I was surprised that no one had come out or asked what was going on. I suppose people keep themselves to themselves I thought. The hire van arrived to pick us up. The coroner had already been called for Dave's one so we made our way to wait outside. Sitting in the minibus everyone was chatting about what they had done throughout during my absence. Nothing too exciting I thought, a very minor car accident and a report for nuisance kids. All of a sudden, I saw a very sick looking ghost like figure walk out of the house Dave was in. Hold on, it was Dave. He really didn't look well. I could see from the minibus that he had rings around his eyes like he hadn't slept for a week and was a very green looking colour.

He came over to the driver's window. I just had to get some fresh air he said. That poor bloke has been laying in front of his electric fire for about a month. I thought he was winding us up but it seemed he was telling the truth. The coroners had arrived and put the bloke in a body bag only for him to disintegrate once inside. Dave said the smell was the worst thing he had ever smelt and the worst thing he had ever seen. Premises secure Dave and his instructor got back on the minibus. What the hell is that? the smell was unbearable. It attacked my nostrils with a vengeance. We better get some air freshener the sergeant said I think this van is being used later. Dave was telling us that the body had rotted and swollen twice its size and was almost becoming part of the carpet. I couldn't help but ask why? Why this man died alone? Why didn't anyone know he died? It's a sad society I thought. Back at the station our day was done. Two days and I've done more than I would ever have expected. I was proud for doing my bit, carrying my fair share of the load. Lying in bed that night the smell of Dave's job still remained. If I ever go to one like that I thought I'm plugging up my nose.

The days and weeks went by. My knowledge was developing, I was getting an understanding. I had learnt so much in such a short space of time. Thrown in at the deep end I thought. Perhaps it done me good, perhaps not, only time will tell. I was coming to the end of my course and everyone was getting a feel for what station they wanted to go to. I didn't really mind they were all convenient to get to. Sitting around the table the sergeant joined us. Do you know that you have got further exams every month, only a few and they will be at your station he said? We all looked at each other with blank looks on our faces. No sarge Paul said. Oh, well every month you have got an exam and you all need to pass or you could potentially be back kicked out he said. Oh, brilliant I thought, more exams. I don't remember anyone telling us about that. Weeks of training and still more tests. My binder was already looking full and I don't think much more could fit inside.

James, the sergeant said. You are going to one of the smaller teams in the district. It's a hard-working team and very busy. You have achieved the most arrests over the course so this is where you're going. These weeks flew by. My kit had started to look worn, boots scuffed and my kit bag was over flowing with paperwork that needed completing. Policing was a tough game and don't let anyone tell you otherwise.

I was honoured with a few days off. It gave me time to reflect on what I had just done and what lay in store with my new team. I couldn't stop thinking about my new station and what my team would be like. It was a Tuesday when I started, early turn. I had a terrible night's sleep and decided to get up at 4am. There was nothing on the roads, the odd bus and the occasional car. Arriving at the station I was so nervous that I drove into the wall of the car park. Just a little scratch but it was the least of my worries. I urgently needed a morning poo and couldn't even get in. the yard was empty and no one answered the buzzer. About 5.30am I saw a couple of other cars arrive. Here we go I thought. Alright mate I said as a tall dark-haired bloke got out of his car. Are you early turn here today I said lacking confidence? Well I hope so, are you James he said? I heard you were starting today. Come with me mate and I'll show you the locker room.

Following on like a lost sheep I noticed the building was yet another old one, I could hear the humming of an old heating system and the smell of cleaning products as I walked up the stairs. There were only a few offices and a very tiny parade room with a table and a charger for the radios which were all flashing green and yellow. Once you get changed mate meet back in the parade room he said. Oh, by the way I'm Tony he said. Nice to meet you I replied….

Ready for work I walked into the parade room. There was about five of us and the sergeant. Welcome James the sergeant said. Right, so your first job is to make the tea he said. Sadly, this is your job until the next new person arrives which is about a year away he laughed. I didn't mind. I expected this. The new boy makes the tea. It was the same wherever you went. As I left the room I heard Tony shout that he likes chocolate biscuits too. Biscuits too I thought but if I am going to be excepted then this is the way forward. I will be learning from my team and will probably be a pain in the back side for them but I will work hard and do my best to get along.

Tea made the postings for the day were read out. James, you will be in the reporting car for some time to get you used to all the report writing the sergeant said. No problem sergeant I said. Just call be skip or sarge mate, it sounds better he said. OK skip thanks. you'll be with Richard the skipper said as Richard held his hand out. Richard was an elderly chap who never had any sense of urgency about him. Richard walked out into the yard and I followed. There it was, our chariot, well a 1.2 litre ford fiesta. Go grab your kit and we'll go straight out he said we've got two calls already. I never did have time for a poo.

The first house we went to was to report damage to a car that was caused by a neighbour's kid. I always remember it. According to the call list they seemed like decent people, although they lived in an area with a playing field opposite their house. Richard knocked on the door. It was about 7am at this point. No lights on and there was silence throughout the house. Another knock, then another and an upstairs light came on. Who is it? a female shouted. It's the police can you come to the door Richard said. A shabby looking lady opened the door, hair all over the place and looking like she was ready for a fight. Yeah what? she said. We are here about the damage to your car Richard said. You are having a laugh aren't ya. You wake me up at 7 o'clock in the morning for this, you're taking the mick she said. What a lovely welcome I thought. I just stood there, not really knowing what to say, well I knew what I really wanted to say but couldn't. We get given the job and we turn up Richard said. If you don't want us to report it then we will go. This lady burst into a barrage of abuse telling us that if we sorted the kids out then there wouldn't be a problem. We are useless, a waste of time, incompetent and she pays our wages. Ok, Richard said, we are off then goodbye. The lady slammed the door so hard it was probably heard a mile away. Don't let people dictate to you about what's what and definitely don't listen to that abuse from anyone. If she doesn't want to report it then what more can we do he said? Job one resulted. Uncooperative female slammed door and didn't want to report.

Where we off to now I asked Richard? Richard wore reading glasses and it seemed like an eternity waiting for him to get them out, open the case, put them on and it irritated me slightly but I would never say anything. We are off to…. a three-day old domestic call. The female's partner had turned up drunk and was banging on her door. Well he isn't going to be there now I thought. Arriving at the new address, again in darkness with a dimly lit communal light outside, it was intercom access. Number 12 buzzed, no answer. We tried a few other flats and an unhappy resident buzzed us in. Walking along the darkly lit corridor I noticed little cupboards beside each front door. What are they for mate I asked? That's for meals to be handed through I think Richard replied. I sucked up my surroundings and thought that this doesn't look like an old people's home and I think it's more for security, but again I never said anything. There were a few that were open and some completely ripped off. Number 11 was ripped off so you could literally see into the living room. As I walked past, well, I had the fright of my life. As my eyes glanced over into this little hole I saw a head. Morning officer the head said. The head was poking so far in, the bloke could have climbed through it. After I composed myself I replied…. morning and walked past. This place is like one of those joke houses you get at the funfair I thought. A knock at number 12 and again no answer. Is this a regular thing I asked? Yeah, but we have to attend. Go away it's too early a distant voice from inside said. It's the police can you come to the door. No, I'm in bed the voice replied. Are you alone inside and are you ok? Well of course I'm OK I was asleep until you woke me up! Charming I thought, these people call us to abuse us. We need to make sure and see for ourselves so can you come to the door please. Oh, for god's sake, that's all I heard, then some banging and clashing then the door swung open. See I'm fine she said. She looked like she had been up for a week. There's no one here so can you please go away and slammed the door. There was a reoccurring theme here. Job two resulted – uncooperative female, told to go away. Safe and well. Right mate, let's go for some breakfast.

The canteen was the hive of activity and wind ups. It was here that I would learn job related phrases like ESSO (**E**very **S**aturday & **S**unday **O**ff) and POETS (**P**$ss **O**ff **E**arly **T**omorrow's **S**aturday) day. It was loud and I noticed everyone sitting together. You getting the teas in then James someone said, I didn't know who. Mine's a tea, and me, coffee please. Bloody hell I ended up buying about ten teas that morning before I even ordered my cheesy beans on toast. The worst thing I done was leave my stuff by the table including my pocket book. My urgency for the toilet had past so I may as well eat I thought. The canteen staff were old ladies, very friendly and from their vast experience didn't take any crap from anyone although they did like flattery. Are you new love one said, yes sweetheart I replied. Sweetheart, oh aren't you lovely. That was the ice broken with the canteen girls, an extra rasher of bacon when I want it I thought. I was a little nervous sitting down. There were coppers from all the other stations there too. I could sense that I was being spoken about, looked at and analysed. It did feel awkward, normally I'm quite sociable but it was too soon to be me, until I looked in my pocket book and saw the biggest penis and pair of breasts. Ten pages were tattooed with body parts and tea stains. I saw the funny side and everyone laughed. After Refs as it's called, we answered a few other calls then it was home time.

My dad was not getting any better. He had been admitted to a specialist Hospital. The brain tumour had grown and there was nothing that could be done. I remember talking to the consultant with my brother. Unfortunately, we are unable to give an exact time frame for your dad but with this aggressive tumour it could be days or weeks he said. At that point my world stopped. I was numb, devastated, heartbroken and being eaten up from inside. My mum didn't come in and I couldn't bring myself to discuss the conversation I just had. Deep down she knew that her soul mate was fading away but she stayed strong. My dad returned home and into the care of my mum. The days and weeks went by and nothing was changing, so much so that I began to convince myself that my dad would pull through and get better. My team were brilliant, really helpful. They knew what was happening. I was the new bloke on team and part of me felt that I was taking the mick. It was an early turn when I got the call. My dad was fading away and I needed to get home fast. It took about 15 minutes before I arrived. My brother and sister were there already and a few other family members. My dad was in the front room in bed, awake. His family were by his side and he could acknowledge us. I could see he was fading. We were rubbing his hands and arms. Its OK dad don't worry we were saying. My tears were never ending. I couldn't talk. We are all here dad then…. his eyes closed for a brief second then they opened once more. The most beautiful crystal blue eyes, one last look at his wife and what they created together then they closed. My dad had passed away with his family by his side. It breaks my heart even to this day and I sneak away to have a little cry every now and again on my own. I need to be strong for my family, our family now. The funeral directors arrived and my dad, for the last time, was lead through his garage where for decades he built, created and found peace with himself. Alright J he used to call me. The smell of rolled tobacco always reminds me of him whenever I smell it. He was a proud man, a family man, a friend to many. He was my dad.

Returning to work was strange. I was feeling weak and tired and at times thought that I had returned too early. In actual fact work was the best thing for me. It allowed me to focus my mind on other people that needed my help. The shoplifters, domestics and missing people were becoming second nature and I was well on my way to completing everything that needed doing. The tests were going well and I was passing those exams too. The more I worked the more I was noticed so the worst jobs were being given to other people.

Can I have a unit to assist me please I heard an officer say over the radio. I was nearby so popped along. I had been given a driving course which allowed me to drive the little cars now so at least I was mobile. I wasn't allowed to drive on blues and twos but I didn't mind. What's up mate I said as I approached the officer? I was quite surprised with what he said. Alright James, I'm not sure but do you think this bloke is dead because he is moving? Having a few seconds thought I asked what he meant. Well, I got called to a sudden death and got inside. I saw the bloke hunched over in the corner of a room but he's moving but looks dead. I didn't want to touch him he said. Right ok mate let's go take a look. That smell hit me straight away. The smell of rotten death, decomposition and flies were everywhere. Mate, this isn't looking too good I said. I walked into a tiny room full from floor to ceiling with thousands of books and magazines. True to his word in the corner was a semi naked chap hunched over and wiggling about. Not much but he was moving.

This is an awful situation to be in I thought. I could feel the smell starting to attach itself to me. This will be with me for weeks I thought, thanks. Putting my gloves on I put my hand on this bloke's shoulder. It was cold, soft and discoloured. As I pulled him back the reason for his wiggling became apparent. The noise sounded like ripping the skin from an orange, that crunchy squishy noise. This bloke had been there so long, undiscovered, that what seemed like an entire nest of maggots had set up home inside his chest cavity. There were thousands of them moving around, exploring, eating and causing him to look like he was moving. It was disgusting, traumatising and I genuinely felt sick. I was there for my dad and no one was here for him. I stepped back and told the officer that he was well and truly deceased. My god he said, is that real, can that happen he said. Well I'm no expert I said but you can see for yourself. Na, you're alright I'll just stand over here. I didn't hang about. I needed some fresh air fast. Back outside I left the officer to deal with all the other paperwork bits that needed doing and I went back to the station because the smell of the house was on me. On my way back to the station I saw blue lights in my rear-view mirror. It was a traffic car. I pulled over as it shot past me like a missile. Then there was another one rocket past me so fast that it shook my car. There was a chase down the road I heard over the radio. I wanted to join in but I was only a reporting car and wasn't allowed to use blue lights or sirens. As I got to the bottom of the road the traffic cars had stopped and were waiting. Then all of a sudden, an old van went past doing about 70mph. They started chasing and it looked brilliant, everyone was looking. It was at that point that I thought. I want some of that. I want to be a traffic cop.

Chapter 6 – I'm not holding out much hope

I regret to inform you that you have been unsuccessful on this occasion. You may reapply after twelve months. I spent hours on that application form. It was the first rejection by letter that I ever had, well since being in the job anyway. Please give me an example of this, please give me an example of how you done that. There were loads of similar questions and I had to write in a certain font size and in so many words why I wanted the job. I thought it was clear cut. You're a hard-working officer, you are never off sick and there are no complaints about you. What's not to want I thought. Clearly it wasn't my time and to say I was gutted didn't even come close. The traffic department was a specialist role. It had to be, I mean advanced drivers, motorcyclists and experts in vehicle examination. Then there was the collision investigation department where they really get their teeth into things. Even my team mates thought I had a good chance. All I ever spoke about was becoming a traffic cop. There was no going back, they didn't want me yet. I had no choice but to knuckle down and do what I do best and police.

My skipper called me in the office. Alright mate. Look I know you're probably disappointed with not getting the job but as a consolation I've put your name forward for an advanced car course. At least with that under your belt you're half way there. Really, cheers skip I replied. It's a long course of intensive driving and it is very hard work, now there's a course in a couple of weeks and I'm trying to get you on that OK he said? Well it was a good pick me up to say the least I thought. As I said my thanks the skipper he told me that I would ruffle a few feathers on the team because people have been waiting for ages for this course, but you deserve it he said. You have arrested over 250 people in the last year, robbers, shoplifters, drunks and burglars so if you get any grief point them in my direction.

I remember the horrible journey to the driving base, it took ages. It hadn't changed but this time I was here for a course I really aspired to get. That first time I heard those coppers talking about it years ago and now it was my turn. The days were long and the driving hard. How these instructors do this on a daily basis was beyond me. I started my course with two others and within the first three days we lost one because they weren't up to scratch. The constant commentary while driving supersonic was tough. The instructors knew it could be done but it went down to those who had the guts to stick it out. Keep it going, keep it going and don't ease off I recall the instructor shouting. I was brushing 150mph and the long sweeping bends were looking more like right angles. My palms were sweating and I thought I was going to die. I was in control, and my life was in my hands. Well done mate, good drive he said as we came back to a realistic 70mph. If you drive to the system then there will be no problems he said. I think it was about the third week and we lost one more so it just left me. The last week was constant driving as there was no one else to swap with. I must have driven hundreds of miles and at light speed. Well that was your final assessment and I'm please to say you passed. I had done it, passed the course. There was always a stigma attached to the advance drivers on team. You even had your own table in the canteen. Well so they said....

Back on team it was a delight to get the keys to a lovely BMW 5 series. I had a new bloke out with me that night. A giant of a man, easily 6,6 and 20 stone. I knew he had my back. Can I have a unit to attend please. We have had a report of a collapsed male outside a block of flats and he is believed drunk the dispatcher said over the radio. Come on mate we will take that. It was my first blue light run in the big boy car and as we arrived on scene I remember that I could only park in a little car port a hundred yards or so away from the location. Show us on scene mate I said. I looked over and could see the silhouette of a person on the floor. As we walked closer and closer I noticed a plain clothes unit coming in from the other side of the block. I think this bloke dead I said. How do you know that the new bloke replied? Look at the way he is laying. My fears were confirmed when I got closer. Mate I'll get on to the ambulance service and you start CPR. This bloke had horrendous injuries. His foot was up by his head and he was bleeding from every orifice. A paramedic arrived and hooked him up to various lifesaving equipment. The plain clothes officers started setting up a cordon for me. He looks like a jumper the paramedic said. I looked up at the tower block and I could see that the window on about the 23rd floor was wide open which I now know was irrelevant. Whatever went on in this bloke's life caused him to end it I thought, or was he pushed? The new bloke was getting more and more covered in blood the more chest compressions he was doing. The blood was spraying everywhere. He looked like a victim himself. We've got a pulse but I doubt he will make the paramedic said in a hurried tone. It looks like he has broken every bone in his body. A bigger ambulance arrived and the bloke was scooped off and rushed to hospital with us right behind. The detectives were at the scene trying to piece together what really happened. Arriving at the hospital he was taken straight to the trauma room where a group of doctors were waiting. In the light the true extent of his injuries was apparent. Clothes cut off I noticed he had horrific injuries from head to toe consistent with jumping from a height but he had holes all over his body, like bullet holes. The doctors went to work and started slicing him open and putting tubes in here and there. This is while a nurse was doing chest compressions. The floor was covered in blood and blooded clothes. There were wrappers of medical equipment stroon across the bed. This bloke's life was almost over there's no coming back from this I thought. They were trying but their efforts were in vein. Are we all agreed the consultant said. Time of death 23.34. I looked at the new bloke. He had only been here three days and this was his first proper job. He had blood on his face, clothes and hands. It was everywhere. Come on mate lets go get you cleaned up and take you back to the station. I could see his suffering, his emotions being held in. It had affected him. Perhaps not tonight or tomorrow but it will. I found out later that the detectives were in investigating a murder as things weren't adding up. The bloke was murdered elsewhere and dumped. He didn't even jump, they were crush injuries after being shot.

I had re-lighted my fire after it simmered out because of my rejection. I was running about answering more calls. I was really enjoying myself, although week by week the days started to repeat themselves and the jobs were very alike until.... All cars wait...I graded call to a multiple stabbing. There are several calls coming in for this. Ambulance service being called the dispatcher said. I was with a bloke called Chris. He had been in about a year or so. Mate we got to go to that I said. I was in the fast car so was expected to get there first. It was a bit of a ride, right over the other side of the ground. I heard another unit arrive on scene as they were literally just around the corner when the call came out. I could hear the panic in the bloke's voice. I need help quickly; this man is bleeding to death he said. Hearing that makes you go the extra mile. Your colleague needs help so you rush to help. The car performed well and I arrived in a few minutes.

There is another person down the road the officer said. I left Chris with this officer. The bloke looked in a bad way. I could see the blood from the car, the pavement was covered in it. There were dozens of people about screaming and hysteria was everywhere. I shot down the road, the radio was constant with officers talking about people they found with various injuries. This sounded like a gang fight gone wrong. I couldn't see anyone. I went up and down a couple of times until in the shadows I saw a person standing there. I screeched to a halt and ran over. The person was clearly in shock but I didn't have time to comfort them. A few yards in front on the pavement was a man dying. He had been shot and blood was everywhere. There were a few nosey neighbours that came out to the noise of my sirens but that's it. I need some scissors quickly so grabbed hold of a pair in my first aid kit. I needed to cut everything off this bloke so I could see what I was dealing with. Clothes off the bloke was in semi consciousness. He had been shot several times. There were little holes everywhere. My hands were shaking but it felt like I went into over drive. I was plugging holes left, right and centre constantly talking to him. His stomach was covered in holes bleeding everywhere. The ambulance arrived and they left my dressings on and picked this bloke my up and went straight to hospital and I went with them. You have probably saved this blokes life the paramedic said. You have stopped the bleeding but he is bleeding inside. Arriving at the hospital he was rushed straight into surgery. It was hours later that a surgeon appeared. Hello officers who found him he asked? Me, I replied. Well, by stopping that bleeding and plugging those holes you definitely saved his life. We had to remove a few bits and he had some internal injuries but nothing we couldn't fix. He was lucky and owes you his life because without your intervention he would have bled to death the surgeon said. I was so tired after working a double shift I didn't have time for praise. He will live to see another day I thought and we left.

Apparently, this bloke had nothing to do with the fight but was in the wrong place at the wrong time.

Being the advanced driver on team the job had its perks. Very rarely would you be given the long drawn out boring jobs that everyone tried to avoid. If anything, you were asked politely to attend a call, if you weren't busy. This was all great until the car broke and I had to resort to driving the station van. The van was a completely different ball game. Running around picking up prisoners and the occasional call in-between. Generally, I was posted on my own in the van and trying to get the thing to go fast was a joke and if you took your foot off the accelerator you were back to square one again. Hosing out the sick from the cage was an unpleasant task too.

Niggling at the back of my mind was being a traffic cop and I still really wanted to do it. I bit the bullet and drove to the traffic base. It looked like a scary place. All the big cars and bikes were there. Everyone dreaded a traffic sergeant because they had the authority to take your police driving permit away from you and I had to track one down. Hello skip as I was walked into the office. We address sergeants as sergeants here he replied looking at me like I had just reversed into his car. Sorry Sergeant I replied. I explained my situation and asked if I could go out with the traffic officers to further my knowledge. What a change in personality. Of course you can mate, no problem he said. Let me know what dates you can do and let me know and I'll sort it out. Thanks sergeant. I had taken the effort and it paid off.

Getting back in the van the weather had taken a turn for the worst. It was quickly turning into a blizzard. A freak snow storm had suddenly overpowered the country. The calls didn't stop and everyone was doing their best to get to them but it took time. Can I have a unit please to a believed collapse behind locked doors. A concerned neighbour has reported not seeing their neighbour and his dog is continually barking the dispatcher said over the radio. It took me about 30 minutes to get to the address. A lovely little house in a quiet cul-de-sac on the outskirts on the ground. The snow had settled on the surrounding fields and looked like a Christmas card. Arriving on scene I remember struggling to get the van up the road as I was skidding and sliding everywhere. I spoke with the neighbour and could hear the dog barking. Hello it's the police can you hear me I shouted through the letterbox. There was nothing, no reply and no horrible smell. Perhaps this bloke has just had a fall I thought, hopefully. In the van I had a piece of kit that we use to smash doors in like a battering ram. It was really heavy yet effective. My first swing and the entire door frame almost come off, then the second and I was in. It's the police are you OK? There were actually two dogs there. I didn't know what they were, they were cross breeds but with what I didn't know. They were big but friendly and happy to see someone. The house was lovely, clean and well kept.

Walking through the address I had that feeling that someone was going to jump out on me again. I couldn't see anything untoward or any smells that would raise my suspicions. I walked into the front room and oh my god, there he was. I needed a moment. A moment to reflect what I was actually witnessing. He was dead without question but had no arms. Everything on both sides was missing. I walked closer and noticed that most of his left shoulder was gone too. There was no blood, just what surrounded him on the sofa which had dried out, no signs of a struggle nothing. I updated my control room and asked for my skipper to pop down. I needed to secure the dogs because I didn't want them escaping into the blizzard. My skipper said it would take him a few hours because the weather was so bad. I lead the dogs into the kitchen area and it was there that I saw a bone in their bed. At first glance it looked like a dog bone but then I noticed it had a flap of skin attached to it. I couldn't take in what I was dealing with here. I was on my own and dealing with a horror story. Have these dogs eaten their owner? I went back to the front room to look over the body. I had to as it was my job and if there was anything evidential I needed to secure it. I put my gloves on and turned the body over to make sure there wasn't any other wounds but there wasn't. There were teeth marks all over the body. How long has he been here for his dogs to eat him I thought? It must be recent because the place didn't smell.

I went back outside to speak with the neighbour and informed her that sadly he had passed away. When did you see him last, I asked? Well about a week or so. I normally see him once a week at least she said. Do you know if he was fit and well I asked? Oh no she replied, he was always on medication and going to the chemist. His dogs were his life she said. Going back inside I thought about what she said. His dogs were his life but his dogs may have taken his life. An ambulance officer waked up to the address holding what equipment he could. I couldn't get the ambulance up here he said. Leading him inside he was as shocked as I was. Together we started looking around for medication to try to aid our investigation as to why and how he died. There were bags of it, some not so important but some was. Ah, the ambulance bloke said. If he needs this then chances are his heart has stopped. It wouldn't cause him to die but it would put him into a coma type environment and he wouldn't be able to move he said. What so he was awake I replied? Quite possibly, sometimes you can go into a state of paralysis he said.

So, it was beginning to look like he didn't take his medication and collapsed and couldn't move. His dogs got hungry and began to eat him. Then as a result of this he bled to death. He was aware his dogs were eating him and couldn't do anything about it. They even licked up every bit of blood. It was like this bloke had just been placed there. The dogs were so friendly you would never have thought it. The snow was not easing and it must have been a good foot deep.

No one could get to us and we couldn't leave. The skipper was still ages away so I couldn't contact the coroner until he got there. So, there was me, the ambulance bloke had to leave but where to I don't know. Perhaps the main roads weren't that bad.

Whatever the environment I needed stay where I was. I wouldn't leave him as he had been through enough I thought. I'm not a religious man but something told me to say a prayer and ask the man upstairs to look after him. I've never told this before but this was to be something I would always do when dealing with a death. It took about four hours for my Sergeant to arrive and another three hours before the coroner arrived to take this bloke away. I had to arrange urgent kennel care for the dogs too and that took another couple of hours. That was another double shift over and done with and the next day will be back to normal, hopefully….

The next day I came into an email for the traffic sergeant asking if I was available for any day next week? I'm not but I can be I thought. I replied quicker than my fingers could type. Sergeant I would be happy to attend a couple of days next week I said. He must have been in the office because I got a reply straight away. Next Tuesday late turn 14:00 he replied. My skipper approved it with no issues. Tuesday arrived and I got to the traffic base at 1pm. A little early I know but you can't knock good time keeping. I logged into my emails to see that I had been told that I am working New Year's Eve. Oh, that's just great I thought, public order team for New Year's Eve. It brings nothing but grief. Hello mate are you James an oldish looking bloke asked? I shook his hand and he told me what the plan was for the day. You will sit in the back and if you have any questions then ask he said. I felt like the new bloke again but I didn't mind as long as it gets me the job.

Squeezing into the back of the traffic car I was immediately taken back how clean it was. I was used to sweet wrappers and coffee cups on the seats. The radio was quiet with the occasional circulation about a stolen car or obstruction. My radio was always constant. I'm liking this already I thought. We started off stopping a few cars, something I never had time to do because I was always rushing about answering calls. These criminals need to get about one of the blokes said and it's our job to stop them from getting to where they're going. He's got a point I thought. I was surprised how many motorists drive without a licence or insurance as we had about three within the first hour. Can I have a traffic unit to a serious collision involving a car and motorbike the dispatcher said. We took the call and were off. I always remember the sirens were different to ours and their cars were more powerful and things just seemed more urgent. We arrived on scene and I was going to jump into action until one of the blokes told me to stick to his side and watch what he does. I saw a car with its front completely ripped off and what looked like a motorbike about 100 yards down the road. The ambulance service was dealing with the motorcyclist. His leathers were all cut off, good ones too, but that was the least of his worries. His right arm was sliced open from his shoulder to his elbow and his left leg didn't look great either. You could see the bone and fatty flesh all exposed. He was screaming in pain and understandably so. They used some drugs to knock him out so they could deal with him easier.

Right, let's see what happened here then the traffic officer said. He started marking up the vehicles with special yellow crayon and measuring various points where the vehicles were. When we looked at the car it looked like it was opened like a can of beans. The motorcyclist had collided side on. In the crumpled metal of the wing was a chunk of the biker's flesh that had been ripped off when they collided. It couldn't be touched as it was wedged in. Someone had jumped the lights but who? OK, we will get an update from the ambulance crew but at the moment It doesn't look like he will die from his injuries so I don't think it will be for us to investigate he said. Not for us to investigate, this looked bad enough. How bad is bad then I thought? The ambulance crew did say that the motorcyclist will live and will recover in time, so we helped move the car and bike and local officers took over. We were there a couple of hours but it seemed like minutes. How long can you expect to be dealing with a fatal collision then I asked? it's not unusual to be there between 6-8 hours. Everyone has to be there he said, collision investigators, detectives and road closures need to be in place. My skipper called my mobile and told me that I couldn't do tomorrow as a couple of officers on my team had gone sick so they needed me back. It is what it is I replied. We made our way back to the base for a break and never went out again because there was paperwork to write up. What a luxury I thought although we got uninsured drivers off the road and went to a serious collision. It was an enjoyable day.

Well New Year's Eve was soon upon me. That time of year that everyone looked forward too except me and my colleagues. It was a minimum double shift and the constant battle with drunks and party goers wanting their photograph with you. I'm not allowed to celebrate the new year or Christmas. Don't get me wrong it's what I signed up to do but you give up important times in your life to police and make people safe. Trying to get the night off was virtually impossible. The more skills you had the less chance you had. Tonight, I would be in my riot kit. My all in one overalls with plastic rubbery protection on all my joints and vulnerable points and a massive helmet. You sweat standing still let alone running. There were quite a few of us, dozens in fact so the chances of getting into serious bother were limited as we would be a wall of blue. My team and a few others were positioned on a pinch point where people were known to rush through at the stroke of midnight to watch the fireworks. I couldn't see any clocks or watches as my eyes were in front watching the crowd. We were there for hours watching the sober become drunk and loud. You couldn't hear your radio so you were reliant on a tap on the shoulder or watching the officer next to you. There were thousands of people. The crowd was hostile before midnight because it was my fault that they weren't allowed through and I was ruining their celebrations. Yeah, because I really want to be here I thought. The sound of smashing bottles and cheers from the crowd were growing so I knew it was getting close. The countdown begun 10-9-8-7 you get the idea. At the stroke of midnight, the street lamps were darkened by the hale of bottles and street furniture thrown in our direction. I could hear the bangs from the fireworks but was using my shield to protect myself from the endless hatred we were presented with. The abuse was nonstop and the pushing and shoving began. Someone in the crowd must have spread the word to urinate in glass bottles and throw them at us. I remember one smashing on my shield and the instant smell or someone's bodily fluid covering my visor and clothes. We were all in the same boat. For a brief second, I recall looking into the upper windows of a building and seeing the colours of the fireworks exploding into the night sky. Happy new year I thought silently. Then back to work. This went on for about 30 minutes and I was seriously knackered. My kit was dirty and drenched and I didn't want to give up and let these hooligans win so I kept going pushing and shouting while the bombardment continued. Then all of a sudden it stopped, the shouting stopped and the crowd dispersed. It was like some had sent a text to say let's go home now. The devastation was noticeable when the street emptied. I wouldn't want to be cleaning this up I thought. It wasn't a big town but everyone from all around had gathered there for years and it had become the annual meeting place. Some officers were worse than others. Some had flour and eggs on them, some including me stunk of urine and some were limping. They had their fun the skipper said. The CCTV will track them down at a later date. Well done you held the line he said. Happy New Year…not even one day off then back in for late shift as we got off at 4am.

I was eagerly waiting for the job advert to come out again. It had been quite a few months since my rejection and I was growing impatient. The juicy calls seemed to be happening when my team wasn't on duty so we were left with the reporting stuff. Equally as important as a victim is a victim in my eyes albeit it wasn't as urgent to get there. It was a Monday when the advert appeared. Similar format with examples of this and that and references to say you were worthy and recommended. I still had my old application and looking through it I noticed mistakes. I realised where I went wrong and I wouldn't make the same mistake twice. Everything done and signed off I began the wait. The rumour mill says it generally takes a few weeks to find out if I got through the application stage. I done my best to forget about it as it was out of my hands. Dear James, I am pleased to inform you that you have been selected to attend an interview for the position of traffic officer. I couldn't believe it, I had passed the hardest part, well so I thought. I was so excited that I told everyone. Perhaps I shouldn't just in case I failed but so what I thought. I began looking through traffic manuals, traffic books, reporting material to further my knowledge. Very rarely did I ever have time for traffic work on team as I was either at a call or in custody. This is how to weigh a vehicle, this is how to examine a tyre and these are the points to prove for dangerous driving. The list went on. This was a completely different strand of policing to what I have been used to and I wanted to make a good impression. I hadn't worn my tunic since passing out and I hoped that it fitted. It was a little bit tight but wearable. I took ages preparing my uniform, polishing boots and making sure I was well groomed for the big day. The journey was long and the nerves overwhelming but I got there in good time and waited in the canteen. One of the interviewers walked in. James, we are just finishing up then you'll be next he said. I think he was a sergeant but I called him sir anyway as he was in plain clothes, just in case. As I walked in the room my nerves were starting to get the better of me, sweaty hands, butterflies in my stomach and dry mouth. Right, can you give me the definition of burglary please the inspector asked. Burglary? Yes, burglary he said. My head was full of traffic stuff. Err well a person commits burglary if he enters a building as a trespasser and....so on and so on. OK thanks he said. Right, what traffic offences do you deal with in your district and what are the offence codes for them he asked? Well, seatbelts and no insurance I replied. And the offence codes? oh I don't know I replied. I've done my legs here I thought, I couldn't answer a question. OK then when was your last drink drive arrest? Two weeks ago, I said. Right so can you tell me the warning formula? I knew this. I will be reporting you for the question to be considered of prosecuting you for the offence of.... OK thanks he said. He began flicking through paperwork, I assume it was my application form. There was a few more questions about what I do now, then he asked for the tyre pressures on the rear of a fully laden traffic car. 40 psi I replied. Well done James, are there any questions you want to ask he said? The only one I could think of was when will I find out? Within the week he replied. A firm handshake and it was over and a long drive home.

Dear James. Thank you for applying for the role of traffic officer. I am pleased to inform you that you have been successful at the interview stage and further instructions will be sent out in due course. May I take this opportunity to congratulate you and wish you every success in your future role. I had done it, achieved my dream job and I was high on life. It was going to be sad leaving my team, my mates and the bond I built over the years but I had to move on. I was going into a specialised role, I was going to be a traffic cop.

Chapter 7 – Why are they called the Black Rats?

So, the day was finally here. I had left my old team and got a good send off. A few bits and bobs and some vouchers. I didn't think I was that popular when I read the card. Walking up to the gate carrying my career in my holdall yet again, I was greeted with another pin code key pad and no intercom. Oh, the joys and memories this brought back. Luckily another bloke was walking behind me so he let me in. I was quite experienced in the job but I was nervous again. I knew I could to the job but it was just getting to know everyone again and making new mates. Walking into the lobby area I didn't have a clue where to go. There were stairs in front of me, offices to the left and right and another corridor leading to god knows where. Shall I stay here or go and explore I thought? I opted to stay put and pretend to look at my phone so it half looked like I was there for a reason other than being lost.

Hello mate do you know where you are going an officer asked? It's my first day mate and I haven't got a clue I replied. Dump your stuff there, we will be parading soon he said, parade room on the fourth floor. Walking up the stairs I noticed yet more old photos and paintings of old traffic cops, old cars to modern day cars. Into the parade room everyone stopped what they were doing and looked at me as I walked in. I think I was the youngest one there. There were quite a few moustaches and beards and a few big bellies. Hello I said. I didn't get much of a response but it was expected. They didn't know me and they didn't have to if they didn't want to. It was down to me to break the ice. Two Sergeants and an Inspector walked in the room and sat at the front facing us. I just want to welcome the new bloke, James, on team the Inspector said. If you see me after parade James we will have a chat. Everyone started jeering like I was in trouble or something and I could feel myself going red. OK sir I replied.

So, James the inspector said, we've got a few things to do before you can go out. I've got you a radio and a locker but we need to talk about getting some courses for you so you can ride the bikes and answer calls on the motorways. Ride the bikes I thought, I didn't think I would be doing that for ages. OK Sir, will I be going out with someone I replied? Of course, you will be with an experienced officer for a few weeks to show you the ropes and the motorway junctions he said. We cover an enormous area about eight times bigger than what your used to and that's why we have got the faster cars. My kit put away I was introduced to my trainer. First impressions were that he looked like a nice bloke. Alright mate, I'm Robert, well Rob, pleased to meet you he said as I shook his hand. I've got a car, let's go for a drive he said. Sitting in the front seat of the traffic car Rob was rustling through his bag. Oh, here it is he said this is yours. In a clear plastic cover, he handed me a white cap cover. Your traffic now mate so you will need to put this over your other one. I hardly ever wore my hat on my old team but this was like a status symbol. The white hat that stood out from the crowd and recognised by everyone. So, Rob, I've been meaning to ask, why are we called the Black Rats I asked? Well he said, there are many reason's but the most common one is because black rats eat their young, it means we even give tickets to our colleagues, no one gets let off. Bet that goes down well I thought, but the laws the law and all that, we're not exempt.

We were driving around for hours and I was trying to absorb all these new places and points of interest. Right rob said, let's do some seatbelt tickets have you got any he asked? Have I got any I thought? I remember a few years ago seeing some tickets at the bottom of my bag until I went to get them out. They were so old they had stuck together and were useless. Well that's put an end to that rob said. Just make sure you have a healthy supply of everything he said. In the car one of us would listen to the local radio and the other to the traffic channel. A call came out that someone had fallen onto the tracks at a station we were about two minutes from. we're nearby rob said we will go. As I arrived at the station everything seemed normal. We were quickly joined by local units and we all made our way to the platform. A member of staff told me that someone had jumped in front of the express service on platform two. There was nothing there, no blood or people running around screaming. I could see the train had stopped away from the station by some distance. I began walking along the platform with rob just in case we saw anything. Half way up I saw a foot on the track, then an arm and a little further up what looked like the persons inside spread along the track. There were more body parts everywhere until I got to the end of the platform. This isn't a job for us rob said. We will help close the station down and cordon it off but transport police are on their way he said. OK mate I replied. I couldn't help but think that this person must have been in such a bad place and had nowhere to turn. I said my little prayer under my breath and we walked back to the car. We may as well start heading back now rob said. Tomorrow I will test you on those junctions….

Day two arrived and rob was asking me where certain junctions were. I didn't have a clue, I really didn't, the area was just so big. I made sure I had a stock of tickets and all the other bits and bobs I needed. The problem was I wasn't trained in anything and most of the stuff I would be dealing with required a specialist technical statement. It would take time but I would get there in the end. let's go and sort your courses out rob said otherwise it'll never happen. I spent a few hours back at the base getting ticked off for various training that I needed.

I didn't work with Rob again and I was posted with this other bloke. It was interesting working with different people. Learning about their lives, their family and their problems. On occasion it felt like we all offered advice to each other about life choices, financial problems and partners. Working long hours, your colleagues were your family. There wasn't much time to seek outside advice and guidance. I've heard it all over the years and tried to help out when I could. Craig was his name, a gentle giant. He was the most chilled out officer I had ever worked with. His outlook on life was inspirational. Live for today mate, look at what happens around you every day he said. Look at these people that leave their families every morning and never return. He went on. Life is fall of what if's. What if I didn't ride my bike today, that lorry wouldn't have hit me or what if I left two minutes later that car wouldn't have killed me. He made valid points. All I'll say James is never say the Q word (quiet), because it generally brings and end to any silence. On que, the radio silence was interrupted. It was strange, not as strange as the next job. A cow and walked into the motorway followed by the entire herd. It was causing absolute chaos. We past on the other side of the road and saw miles upon miles of traffic and right at the very front was indeed about twenty cows. It took us ages getting through the traffic but we got to the front. Everyone looking at us thinking we had an immediate remedy. The jokes started over the radio. Do you need a hand mooooving them out the way and it's and udder nightmare job. What we doing with this lot then Craig I asked? He looked at me with a blank look on his face. Perhaps get clumps of grass he replied. Between us we didn't have a clue. Policing was about thinking on your feet. The motorway tail back was at least ten miles long. I walked through the broken fence and hiked about a mile across the swampy field and knocked at this little house. I was absolutely smothered in wet mud. An old boy opened the door and knew straight away. They haven't got out again have they he asked? Yes mate, and they are causing mayhem on the motorway. What my chickens he said? Your cows I said firmly. The fence is broken and the entire herd is grazing on the hard shoulder. We both jumped in his little 4x4 and made our way back across the field. The cows knew his whistle straight away and began walking back into the field like they knew it was home time and they were in trouble. The bloke couldn't be more apologetic. We had made the news when the traffic began to flow again. It's one of those things I thought, it happens. The main thing was no one, animal or person was hurt. We were in the road for hours dealing with that job as motorists were breaking down in the queue too. Back to the base for a well earnt cup of tea. How ironic when I looked in the fridge and we didn't have any milk!

A few weeks went by and I was standing on the steps outside when I saw a bloke walking towards me. He had that new bloke look about him, but the biggest giveaway was he was carrying his career on his back too.

Alright mate I said is this your first day? Yeah, he replied. I asked him what team he was on and he said mine. I'm James as I held out my hand, Martin he replied. Little did I know at that stage that I just found my best mate within the job. I showed him around and sorted a few things out as I knew the people to go to. It made it easier for him and I knew exactly what he was going through. He went through a few weeks training with another officer and it worked out quite nicely that most of our courses were at the same time. Once we got our basic courses out the way I think the supervisors noticed that we were getting on really well and they posted us together every day. We were smashing the tickets out and arresting loads of bad guys. It was like I was on my old team again but our playground was a lot bigger. We were getting a name for ourselves and really beginning to shine and get noticed by the senior ranks.

We were known as a couple of pranksters so we always tried to live up to our reputation. Here James, what do you think you can do with this Martin said as he held a bottle of ink? Brilliant I thought. Pass me Rob's hat. I proceeded to ink the velvet insert in Rob's hat and put it in his bag. When we were out on patrol I got a call on my mobile. Have you put ink in Rob's hat Craig asked? I don't know what you're talking about trying not to laugh. He's stopped a car and put his hat on briefly but then took it off. He looks like a Ninja he said crying with laughter down the phone. The funny thing is he doesn't even know and the motorist is looking at him and trying not to laugh too! Well, me and Martin had to pull over as the tears and laughter were uncontrollable. To say Rob was angry was an understatement and he swore to get me back but he never did, well apart from turning my locker back to front and padlocking it but I saw the funny side. I never forget Rob shouting out our name's whenever something went wrong. We would periodically do pranks, pretending to be commanders calling the sergeants office, leaving the heater on full in the cars and occasionally draw pictures in pocket books. It made us what we were, a team, and we all had laugh even when we were the ones being pranked.

We hadn't done a big job yet as thankfully no one was getting seriously hurt on our roads. Traffic unit now please, reports of a car fire after a collision the dispatcher said. Person trapped and the fire service are being called. This sounded like a bad one and Martin was driving today. Arriving on scene the fire service was putting the last of the flames out. The smoke was very intense and it filled the entire road. There is one fatality the chief fire officer said, we couldn't get him out. Something drastically went wrong here as the car wasn't smashed up badly and had collided with a bollard at the side of the road. The road was a little cut through and hardly ever had traffic down it. What caused his car to burst into flames and why couldn't he get out? More officers were arriving and closing off the road and moving the public out the way. They shouldn't be seeing this I thought. I don't want to see this either. As the smoke cleared the body of a man was slumped behind the wheel. His body was still smoking and every part of him was burnt off, he looked like a wax model. I could see his teeth and that was it. What a terrible way to die and I owed it to his loved ones to find out why and how this happened. I called the investigators out and the lengthy process began. Enquiries were being made, CCTV viewed, road measured and photographed. It took about seven hours before we could open the road again. It seemed that this poor bloke had a heart attack at the wheel and as he mounted the pavement he somehow split his fuel line which caused the car to burst into flames. Witnesses said that the car was completely on fire within a minute so the chances of getting him out in time were slim. It was a miracle that people weren't walking along the pavement and no one else was killed I thought.

My relationship with Martin had to be suspended for a few weeks as I was given my bike course. Back up to the driver training base again but this time I would be on two wheels. Can everyone tell me about their riding history the instructor said. James, we will start with you. Well, I said, I had a lovely bike once until it got written off because I slid down the road and hit a parked car so I haven't ridden since. Right OK, well if you fall off the horse just jump back on he replied. I wanted to be cut a bit of slack but it didn't seem like I was getting any. Everyone else rode bikes for hobbies and all owned their own. I was thinking I was a bit out of my depth here but I'll give it a go I thought. These beasts were massive, really heavy and weighed a tonne. At some point I had to do a cone course on this. You could just about walk through the cones let alone get that monster through them. I will cross that bridge when I come to it I thought. We started off riding around the training site, riding kerb lines, standing on the seat and doing full lock turns. Everything that was abnormal we had to make normal. I had to be at one with my machine and trust it. My bike was more than capable, but was I?

It was hard riding and we covered hundreds of miles every day. There were a couple of unlucky students that didn't cut the mustard and were kicked off the course. There were a few near misses. 150Mph in the rain on the motorway isn't fun I thought but it proved you had the bottle and were safe to do it. You will drop your bike on this cone course the instructor said and he was right. The first full lock turn was fine, and so was the second then. I had no power, brakes on and I started to tilt. The point of no return was upon me and fell off like a sack of potatoes. Everyone laughed but I'm glad I done it here rather than out on the roads! Get back on and do it again the instructor said. I done it again and was even more nervous than before. The roar of the engine and the burning of the clutch I was getting through it. One more full lock turn then…. done. See its easy when you know how the instructor said. Thank god that was done. That was the make or break part of the course and you had to pass it or your off. Tomorrow would be my assessment and blue light exercise. It was brilliant. My child hood heroes were John and punch from the TV show chips and I was doing what they used to do. I remember as a kid wearing my favourite white shirt with US Marshall's written on it pretending to play chips with my mate Stuart in the playground. I was doing it for real and it was amazing. Well done James the instructor said you've passed. I was chuffed to bits as I was now a proper traffic cop.

Back with Martin he gave me an instruction never to leave him again as he didn't understand anyone else's work ethic. We had been working together and understood how each other worked. If

I'm totally honest he was a very similar character to me. We never argued or disagreed as our thought process was identical. We were poached by other teams and given jobs which required that bit of extra attention to catch the bad people. Although we arrested dozens of criminals we always remembered that I core duty was saving lives. OK, so giving someone a ticket annoys them, but they know they shouldn't speed or use their phone when driving. If they killed someone then it's a completely different ball game. In actual fact I think I was doing them a favour and preventing them from going to prison. I couldn't be everywhere and I only worked a certain number of hours in the day so I couldn't prevent everything.

"Come on mate I said, I always wanted to know how to make chicken tikka". Martin looked at me like I was on something. "Pull over here" I said right outside a curry house. "Wait here mate, I won't be long". I went around the back of this curry house and knocked on the back door. It was about 11am so they weren't open yet. A very old man opened the door a saw a copper standing there. He was even more shocked when I told him that I was there to see how they made their chicken tikka. "come in, come in officer" he said. I think he was hiding something because he was really hospitable. After about thirty minutes I was an expert and knew all the ingredients and how to cook it. "What you got there?" Martin said. "Mate, he cooked us a chicken korma" The only problem was that we didn't have any forks or spoons. It didn't bother Martin. He peeled back the lid and started eating it with his fingers.! You can imagine the mess. It looked like he had put his hands down a dirty drain. "This is lovely" he said. I couldn't help but think of the next driver that is going to touch that steering wheel. "What a winner" Martin said. Well, you got to have some perks I thought.

Emergency call now, elderly female hit by car and CPR is being done by a member of the public the dispatcher said. I knew exactly where this was and it took me a few minutes to get there. The ambulance crew hadn't arrived yet so I immediately took over the CPR on this lady. It was obvious that she had crossed the road and didn't look and was hit by a car. This was someone's nan I thought and I will not let her die. She had a bad injury on her hip but Martin covered this with a trauma dressing. I remember the uncomfortable feeling of crunching ribs as my compressions were acting as her heart. I was doing this for about ten minutes or so until the trauma vehicle arrived with a doctor and paramedic inside. Keep it going officer the doctor said, we need to get our kit out. My arms were numb and I was sweating. Martin was dealing with witnesses and the driver. There were tubes everywhere, wires and monitors all around us. she's got a very weak pulse the paramedic said. I was told to stop and she maintained her pulse although very faint. Right let's stabilise her legs and get moving the doctor said. Can you drive our car the paramedic asked? No problem I replied. The old lady was rushed to hospital and while there began to come around. Will she be alright I asked the consultant? Its early days officer but I hoping she will be. She did pull through and something inside me told me I had to visit her. A few days later I went back to the hospital and saw this frail old lady battered and bruised with her son and daughter beside her bed. Hello, I'm James and this is my colleague Martin I said. We were the officers that helped your mum. Half expecting some thanks the son burst into tears and hugged me. Thanks so much for being there for my mum, she's not ready to leave us yet. We owe you a lifetime of gratitude he said. I could feel my bottom lip starting to go but I took a gulp and said that's what we are here for. We stayed for half hour or so then left. That's what this job is all about I thought, helping people and saving lives.

It seemed that the jobs were few and far between here and you had time to do other things which was good, although when a job did come out you knew it would be bad. Martin and myself were left alone and were dependable. We saw a lot of stuff and could whole heartedly rely on each other inside and outside of work. We needed to because we didn't want to seek comfort from others just in case we came out as weak. I saw death in all forms over the years and it would never stop. I just hope that when my time comes its peaceful and with loved ones by my side like we were with my dad. The months turned into years and people were coming and going, new starters and leavers. The job changed but we never. Martin was like my brother; my back bone and I always knew he would be there for me the same as I would be for him. We patrolled all over and built relationships with various squads and departments.

It was a Saturday morning when my life would change. The job that everyone dreaded. Traffic unit please to reports of a female and child serious collision the dispatcher said. We were literally a minute away and arriving on scene I took a breath. There were people screaming everywhere, people running away. There was debris from traffic lights and railings all over the place. You couldn't begin to imagine the devastation that I was witnessing and we were the first unit on scene. A paramedic arrived seconds after and Martin and the paramedic ran towards the car. Something told me to look down the road, where the car had just come from. I froze, the first time I had ever done that. I remember seeing a person standing on the other side of the road like a ghost just staring clearly in shock. It was like I could hear everything but couldn't take it in. I glanced over and saw the body of a child and the mum. They weren't moving. My mind was begging me not to go any closer as it was scared of what it may remember. I didn't want to be here I thought. I could see that I couldn't do anything. It was obvious to me that they had been killed by the car. I struggled to talk to the control room as I was asking for everything and everyone to get here. I shouted to Martin but he had grabbed hold of the driver who was also injured, slightly. The paramedic ran back to me. I think he could see my distress. He was in shocked as I was. Two professionals looking at two lives that had been taken away. Their injuries were beyond any miracle to repair. More and more officers and ambulances arrived and helped get the situation under control. The driver was drunk and could barely walk even at 8am on a Saturday morning. I had to remember my code, I needed to otherwise I would be out of a job. We must serve everyone without fear or favour and everyone is innocent until proved guilty. Leaving the scene and going back to the base I was surprised how everything was normal further up the road. People going about their daily lives oblivious of what I had just seen. We were both let off early that day, only an hour or so but I can't remember the drive home. All I wanted to do was have a shower. Getting in the hot shower I remember just breaking down. The tears still present themselves as I write. I was hurting, upset and completely broken. That job affected me and still does. A piece of me was lost forever that day and my heart went out to those victims.

I came back to work a different person, a different officer. I tried to put on a brave face but I struggled. I became fearful of every job that came out over the radio. Some officers didn't mind dealing with jobs like that. I always questioned myself and asked if they were stronger than me and were better than me. Everyone has a weak point I kept telling myself and that was mine. I found myself just issuing tickets instead. OK, there was a bit of grief here and there but nothing like what I saw that day. I've dealt with bad jobs over the years and didn't give them a second thought. It was because it was a child and mother in such terrible circumstances that kept playing on my mind. Martin told me that time was the only healer but weeks after I still felt the pain. I got awarded a commendation for that job but why? it wasn't going to bring anyone back. I got a piece of paper and a handshake and they lost their lives.

I went on day by day and the graphic memories were starting to fade. Perhaps time was the only healer after all. But still to this very day I get the occasional flashback and take myself to one side and have a moment to myself, a prayer, a cry, a moment to gather my thoughts. Was my time coming to an end in this role, who knows? All I know is this. I served the job well, I saved lives and I was loyal to my friends. Family and friends can continue to share their lives with their loved ones because of my commitment, my commitment to the oath. No one said policing would be easy and nothing can prepare you for what you will be called upon to deal with. Every job is different, life changing for the person picking up the phone, but just another job for us, a job for us that requires our attention, our code and our compassion. We walk into the darkness when others seek the light. We defend those that cannot defend. We guide those that need guidance and are there when you need us. We offer companionship to our colleagues and cry the same tears. I am proud to wear the uniform and I am proud of its history. I fight on out of respect for my fallen colleagues. I am a police officer, and I am proud.

999 Police.... what's your emergency?

Printed in Great Britain
by Amazon